# STEALING HOME

### D. R. WILLIS

Coffee
&
Kisses
Press

BOOKS BY D. R. WILLIS

*Lonely Shadows*

*Stealing Home*

A short story included in:
*Lacing Words: A Series of Poems and Short Fiction From
Around the World*

TO AVA ROSE

"Pay no attention to the man behind the curtain!"—
L. Frank Baum

The Wonderful Wizard of Oz

# PROLOGUE

*1961 July*

Her eyes were shut tight. Still she knew there was light, there were those voices, and then the overwhelming sense of fear.

Becky Taylor opened her eyes or perhaps they had been open all along. She wasn't quite certain of the order of things. Somehow through her hazed thoughts she knew her body was in the horizontal position with everything around her a blurred grayish-white. Becky became more than disturbed that she could not seem to move. Not an inch. Not at all.

She heard an echoed voice speaking, a voice that was recognizable to her, but try as she might there was no placing a face with it. The familiar sound of it scared her even more than being paralyzed. That didn't make sense. Nothing made sense.

If only the haze could lift then I could remember…anything.

"Her eyes are open. Do you think she's waking up?" the male voice said.

There was already less of an echo.

"No. Shouldn't be. She is on a lot of pain medication," a female voice answered. "I don't want to give you any false hope. I'll call the doctor."

*Doctor*? Becky pondered, as her vision began to gradually clear. Her eyes could make out the unmistakable shape of hospital bed rails surrounding her body. White walls everywhere. Cementing what she had heard.

Why?

She still struggled to remember the beginning point to this madness. But her memory was a maze of faintly opened doors with only darkness peering through.

"Thank you," the male voice said.

*Dammit, that oh so tantalizing familiar voice again.* Fear revealed itself once more.

"The doctor will be here in just a few minutes," the female's voice said. "He's doing his rounds."

"Good, I'll wait."

Becky focused her vision in the direction of the familiar voice. She could make out he was sitting down not too far from her bed. Her eyesight continued to improve by the second. She saw a nurse flittering around the room. And then finally she recognized the man in the chair.

Her memories ripped into her head. She tried to scream to the nurse, get him away from me! Not a sound came out of her mouth. Hell, she couldn't even move her finger to point toward him.

There was a sad, warm smile on the man's face. He was staring right at her. Of course he was.

*Please nurse, help me!* Becky was certain she was able to manage an eye twitch.

The woman wearing the white and blue uniform came over slowly, bending down closer and closer to her patient. The nurse then simply propped another pillow behind Becky's head.

# PART I

*1961 April*

NATIONAL NEWS

One of the top movies of the year
*Breakfast at Tiffany's.*

One of the top books of the year*; Catch-22*
Joseph Heller

LOCAL NEWS

TRAGEDY STRIKES OUR BELOVED MUDHOGS—
*The Farmstead Gazette*

CHAPTER ONE

*Randel Stadium, Northwest edge of Farmstead City, Georgia*

Within the confines of Randel Stadium, the pleasing aroma of freshly mowed grass was still evident in the air as the Mudhogs' championship banners, all five of them, cast flickering shadows onto centerfield like some mesmerizing ballet of motion. Cool prevailing winds that began the day turned to warm ones with late morning rising temperatures taking its usual firm, summer hold. It would have made for a picture perfect day to play Triple-A baseball.

Momentarily lost in her own thoughts, Becky Taylor sat in the stadium's hard, slate gray seat staring up into the vast blue skies. The sun warmed her face, but not her heart. One tear, then another, escaped and she wiped at them quickly. She had vowed not to cry in public knowing full well her own promise would have been impossible to keep. She wiped again at her cheeks with the back of her slender wrist.

Becky felt her arm being poked causing her thoughts to come a screeching halt. Sitting next to her was Donna, the only friend she made in college.

Donna was trying her best to dish out some kind of big sisterly advice. "Forget about whoever this guy was who broke you heart."

Becky didn't retain a single word; it went in one ear and out the other.

Becky had never been very good at sharing personal things with any other living soul, so she kept her rare dating life and Donna at opposite ends. Becky tried to find the right words. "That obvious? It's…just…he left me so suddenly." Another tear slid out; she didn't bother to wipe at this one.

"You'll find someone else. I know you will. Men love pretty and petite," Donna comforted. She then took her hand and gave Becky's shoulder a gentle squeeze. "I only want to see you happy."

"I know you do." Becky nodded her head simply to appease. Wanting to change the subject, she blurted out, "I, I just don't know what to do, Donna, stay here or go back home to New Jersey."

"I can't answer that for you," Donna said. "Not unselfishly, anyway."

They both turned their sights back toward the field. Becky fought not to burst into tears again. If she had slept at all the last couple of nights would she have a bit more control of her emotions. Would the emptiness go away? Would the pain dissipate? *Time heals all things, right?* Although she never found that to be entirely true. Her eyes followed all of the people mulling about on the stadium's grassy field.

A priest steadily made his way through and around the mourners to a microphone stand that was placed between home plate and the pitching mound. Black cables snaked out from the stand, across the field, disappearing down the steps of the first base dugout.

Waiting directly in front of the microphone was a sizable man wearing a charcoal gray suit with a cowboy hat grasped in his hand hanging at his side. His other hand held the stand tightly. "Thank you," his deep voice echoed throughout the stadium. "Thank you everyone for showing your support and love on this very somber day. Father Joe will now take over." He stepped aside, taking a place next to a young woman wearing a fur stole.

The priest unsuccessfully attempted adjusting the height of the stand so he stretched his body enough to bring his mouth close to the microphone.

"Who's the guy who just spoke," Becky whispered quickly to her friend.

"That's the owner, Randel Sawyer, as in *Randel Stadium*," Donna whispered. "And the woman standing next to him, all decked out, is not his daughter, it's his—" Donna stopped talking with the priest's first words.

"Everyone, please rise!" Father Joe said. His short, thin body swayed in front of the stand with both his hands enfolding the microphone. The spectators on the field— most of them baseball players, their wives, and family members in dark clothing—all seemed to freeze into place with the sound of the priest's voice.

Becky stood.

Donna stood then leaned over. "Becky, it'll be okay," she soothed.

Becky faked a smile. "I know. I'm okay already, really." She took Donna's hand and gave it a slight squeeze.

Father Joe began with leading everyone in a short prayer before speaking his rehearsed words. "We are joined here today to remember Richard Robinson and Eddy Walker. Forget for a moment they were exceptional baseball players whose lives were tragically cut short a week ago to this day. Instead, let us remember that they were good, decent family men and above all else, God fearing men. I'm told Richard would have made the majors soon and Eddy would have been a father in only a few short months."

Becky inhaled a sudden breath. Donna and Becky began to cry.

"Oh my God, I feel so bad for Eddy's wife," Donna said.

Becky could only shake her head.

Father Joe continued on at length. His Maine accent combined with the stadium echo made a few of his words nearly impossible to decipher. He spoke about how faith is tested at times like this. How prayer is the answer. How comforting it is to know the two young talented ball players who died in the tragic bus accident are now in a better place.

Becky couldn't help but wonder how the priest could truly believe there could be comfort in his cookie-cutter words for anyone in the player's lives. How the priest could talk with such passion about two people he had probably never met. *Besides, dead was dead. End of story.* She instantly felt horrible about thinking such things.

*A baby coming?*

"Please, bow your heads now so we can have a moment of reflection," the priest concluded.

A few seconds passed by, followed by an awkward splattering of applause from the hundreds of people scattered throughout the lower parts of the stands. The surreal cheering effectively brought an end to the memorial. Nearly everyone started to disperse from the stadium in single file along the thin concrete-stepped aisles with heads bobbing up and down as they moved along.

Becky and Donna remained in the first row near the home team's dugout as they continued peering out toward the congregation on the field. Becky had fixed her sights on one particular person; his head was hanging downward as he steadied himself with the aid of crutches. A moment ago he had hobbled his way over to a man, woman, and child. The man had shaken his hand. The woman, clutching onto the child, seemed to turn away from him.

"The families have to be thinking why, why them?" Becky thought out loud.

"Supposedly, they were the only two sitting at the very front of the bus. I can't imagine what their families must be going through," Donna added.

Becky opened her purse to pull out a pocket sized memo pad and then began to rummage through the rest of her things. "Damnit!" she said, and turned to Donna. "Do you have—" Her friend was already waving a pencil in the air. Becky widened her bright hazel eyes before snatching the pencil from her. "Thanks."

As far back as Becky could remember, she had wanted to grow up to be a reporter, just like Lois Lane. Her dad would tease her that other little girls wanted dolls to play with, she only wanted a typewriter. Of course that wasn't true—well, maybe a little.

"How could you have just graduated college with honors, with two majors, English and Biology, dream of becoming a journalist, and not remember to take something to write with?" Donna said.

Becky could only flash sad eyes back at her apparent teasing.

"You really loved this guy; there's nothing I can do?"

Becky shook her head. "You're really sweet, Donna. But no, it's over." She then watched as the priest gave a pat on the back to the man using the crutches. "Don't forget I wanted to be a doctor too, like my dad. Any idea who the guy is with the crutches?"

"Really, Beck? He's only their number one star player, Joseph Tonti. The Mudhogs' best first baseman ev-er," Donna said. "When he's at bat they chant J-T, J-T, Jaaaaay T." Donna mimicked the cheer. She glanced at Becky's blank expression. "No? Okay, so I'm a Mudhogs fan. Sue me."

"Oh...*that* Joseph Tonti," Becky said as she scribbled a couple of sentences into her memo pad.

Joseph hobbled straight toward the dugout they were sitting behind. Before disappearing down the dugout steps, Becky's eyes met with his and in that brief moment she could have sworn he was going to smile at her. Then he was gone. Becky berated herself for not attempting to at least say a word or two of consolation. She wondered how close he was to Eddy and—it took her a moment to remember the other guy's name—Richard.

"Beck? Becky Taylor!" Donna said.

"Huh?"

"We should go," Donna stated.

"Okay, one more sec," Becky said. She hurriedly finished jotting down some of the key points of the memorial. Somewhere in the middle of her first paragraph she wrote a headline—'Touching moments witnessed by many'. Becky scratched out the line and rewrote it. 'Touching moments at Randel Stadium'. *Better.* She looked briefly at her friend. "Almost done, honest."

"So, Beck," Donna said, "you're still just gonna walk in and submit what you're writing to the Farmstead Gazette?"

"I guess that's still the plan. I have to, so I can at least honestly tell my mom and dad I tried," Becky said.

"It sounds, more and more, like you're going home, no matter what happens at the newspaper?"

"Yeah, I need to be with family, for a while," Becky said. She scribbled down her last sentence. *With crutches in hand, the Farmstead Mudhogs' handsome first baseman's sadness in particular affected the priest the most.* Immediately, she erased the word 'handsome'.

Becky closed the memo pad shoving it into her purse. "Ready."

The two made their way out of the stadium and into Donna's red Cadillac convertible.

With the top down, Donna drove them to a short, dead-end side street where the Gazette's unimpressive, one story brick building stood between two empty lots. A rectangular sign in black lettering saying, FARMSTEAD GAZETTE, was bolted high up on the facade.

Becky crinkled her nose. "What's that smell?"

Donna pointed across the way. Encompassing most of the block was another brick building with a hand written cardboard sign in one of the clouded windows. It read: tool and die. From where they were parked they heard the muffled sounds of machines screeching through stubborn metal.

Becky got out of the car and walked around the hood to the driver's side. For a moment she stood posed underneath her tight pin curled auburn hair, tugging on her grey twill skirt. She bent over and gave Donna a hug.

"So, this is the final goodbye? How will you get back to your apartment?" Donna asked.

"I feel like walking," Becky tried to smile. "It's a beautiful day, right?"

Donna shifted her car into drive. "You know, you kinda look like Lois Lane; only younger and prettier," Donna said.

"And you still look like my best friend," Becky commented. She suspected this could be the last time she saw her freckled faced, red-haired best and only friend.

"I have to meet this best friend of yours. She must be very beautiful," Donna laughed and then began slowly pulling away. "Love you," she yelled.

Becky waved.

Waiting until her friend's car was completely out of sight, Becky began walking away from the newspaper building. She had spotted a pay phone on a corner a block away and there was a call she needed to make.

CHAPTER TWO

Becky stepped inside the cramped, red-striped glass phone booth. Her nose crinkled up for the second time today. She instantly smelled a wretched, soured odor of unknown origin coming from within. She decided keeping the hinged folding door opened was a super idea.

As her hand plunged into the bottom of her purse to feel for a dime, her mom's voice entered her head. *Always have change on you. You never know if you'll need to take a bus or make a phone call.*

*She can never treat me as a grownup, can she!*

Her quick search of the contents of her purse revealed a memo pad, Donna's pencil, a crumpled up five dollar bill, two singles, keys, but no change. *I swear, if you didn't have your head attached to your shoulders, sometimes you'd forget that too.* "I haven't changed in that respect, Mom," Becky admitted.

She rested her purse on the phone's small uneven metal shelf and picked up the receiver to listen. No dial tone. She felt around the bottom of the change container. Empty.

From the corner of her eye she detected a round object lying in the corner, blending in with the metal grated floor. It was a dime. Becky felt like she'd won a jackpot. Putting the somewhat sticky coin into the phone slot, she grabbed the receiver once more-still no dial tone. *Out of order? Really?*

"Can I be of a-sit-mince, ma'am?" a man's voice said from a very close proximity.

Startled, Becky turned. A bearded man stood with blood shot eyes peering down at her. He positioned one foot in and one foot out of the phone booth. She involuntarily gasped. The fronts of his shoes were tearing away in a curl. A collage of stains showed on what she could only imagine might have been a white tee-shirt at some point in time. His protruding stomach was severely testing the limits of his clothes. He swayed back and forth with his right hand grasping the folding door, both anchoring his body down and trapping her.

Becky's heart began to pound considerably, to the point she glanced down at her chest, half-expecting to see movement under her skin. She hadn't thought she could be frightened this easily; she hadn't thought anything could smell worse than the inside of the phone booth— Becky had been wrong on both counts.

"Did you hear me?" he growled. Reeking of a cocktail of liquor and soured things he continued to fidget uncomfortably close.

Becky didn't berate herself for being scared, actually, she hated that besides a good ole shin kicking, she hadn't the slightest clue on what she would do after that, if running away wasn't an option. He was clearly too damn big.

Out of nowhere she spotted a boy on a bike riding in their direction. To her he wasn't merely a strange neighborhood kid-it was a one man, pedaling Calvary. "No-no thanks. I don't need assistance. He's coming to help me," she lied, as she pointed toward the kid on the bike and then did an over-the-top wave hello at the young biker.

The drunken man's yellow eyes darted about and then he simply turned around. Somehow without falling he staggered across the street. An automobile's horn blared, after the car nearly clipped him.

Becky let a breath out as the boy in blue shorts and a yellow striped shirt—who she guessed wasn't much into his teenage years—reached the phone booth. He tried pushing at the kick stand with his foot and then finally he let the red Schwinn bike fall. From the dirt splattered on his legs, one of his activities of the day must have been pedaling through large muddy puddles.

The boy gawked at Becky's pretty face for a moment before speaking. "You okay?"

She kept her sights on the strange man watching him turn a corner and disappear from view. "Yeah, thanks. Thanks for coming over," Becky said.

"My dad says that man is our token homeless guy. Whatever that means," the boy said. "I just think he's a little kooky, is all."

"Well, anyway, thanks," she said, and then added with an outstretched hand, "Hi, I'm Becky."

"Danny," the kid replied. He stuck out his smudged hand and he did one exaggerated shake with a bit of dirt being transferred onto her palm.

"So, Danny, do you know where I might find a phone that works?" Becky said.

"Did you try using a dime?" Danny said.

Becky nodded her head.

Danny smiled, dug into his pocket and pulled out two nickels. "Only the five cent slot works on this phone. I was going to buy a chocolate bar, but here." He extended his hand out to her offering up his two coins.

Becky couldn't help but smile and then the boy's face turned a shade of red.

"Okay, I'll take them, but—" she reached into her purse to grab one of the dollar bills— "you have to trade them for this."

"Wow!" Danny blurted. He started using his fingers to count and then gave up. "That'll buy a lot of chocolate bars. Thanks...Becky." He got on his bike to head straight to the closest newspaper stand. "Maybe catch ya on the flip side." He couldn't wait to find the other kids on his block to tell them about his cute, hep and *older* girlfriend. After he spent his dollar, of course.

Becky immediately put in the nickels and got a dial tone. She sighed.

## CHAPTER THREE

*"This is the operator with a collect call from Becky Taylor; will you accept the call?"* Becky heard the unmistakable drone-like tone of the female operator as she broke down each word into distinct syllables.

*"Henry. Henry, get over to the phone; it's Beck."* Becky recognized the voice as her mother's, even though it sounded as if she was listening through a conch shell.

*"Do you accept the call?"* the operator repeated flatly.

*"Tell our daughter that collect calls cost more than regular calls,"* her father lectured, apparently using the same conch shell.

*"Do you accept the call?"* Some annoyance sneaked through.

"Mom! Just accept the call!" Becky implored.

*"Oh, right. I accept the call, thank you operator,"* Becky heard her mother say with no response given. She guessed that the operator was already two calls ahead.

Becky waited a beat or two for her mom to say something first, but there was only silence as if she wasn't even there at all. "Mom, you can talk now."

"*Hi honey, so how's everything going? I was starting to get a little worried.*" Although tinny, her mother's words were clear enough to understand.

Becky took a breath. "I'm sorry, Mom, that I didn't call yesterday." She paused. "I'm...I've..." A slight but distinguishable sound of a sob came out. Then another. Becky held the receiver away for a moment before bringing it close to her face again. God, everything had turned so surreal and she wondered how long the emptiness would remain. "How is Dad? Has he slowed down any with his practice?"

"*Slowed down? You know your dad, sometimes I think he thinks that life is just one big game. Remember you use to call him the doll doctor because he would stich up your broken dolls. But enough about that, sweetheart, is everything all right?*" her mom said. "*Becky, honestly, is everything all right?*"

*My heart is broken Mom, and there's nothing I can do about it, nothing.*

Becky squeezed the received with her knuckles turning white. "I just miss home, is all, honest." She added vaguely, "You always know when something is wrong, Mom."

"*Sweetheart, I've known you for over twenty-three years. I could tell something has been troubling you from the last couple of calls. Of course that, and the fact I can plainly hear you crying.*" She paused. "*Well, we left your room exactly as it was in case you ever decided to come back home. We did the same thing for your sist—*" Her mom cut off, but it was too late.

"My sister? How is Amelia?"

"*She's doing...well,*" her mom remarked.

"Does she ever ask about me?" Becky nearly whispered. "Has she changed at all?"

Her mom sighed audibly into the phone. "*Be patient, Becky.*"

"Right. Sure. Mom, can you at least tell her that—"

Her mom cut her off. "*Rebecca, all I can say is, be patient.*"

She hated hearing her mom say, Rebecca. She knew it was only used in times of annoyance. "I have to go now," Becky said abruptly, putting the receiver back in place. She couldn't hear another word about being patient. She picked up the dead receiver and talked into it anyway. "So you'll tell my sister I still love her, *thanks* Mom. And yeah, this guy ended up being a jerk and I didn't know it. What did you say? Give the jerk another chance? It's not possible. Yeah, you take care too, Mom." She slammed the receiver onto the payphone. "I loved him," she whispered.

The distinct sound of a bicycle bell cha-chinged from only a few inches away. Still in the phone booth, Becky spun quickly around. Danny was straddling his bike.

"Geez Louise, you scared me!" Becky declared.

"I'm sorry, I'm sorry," Danny burst out, revealing his lisp. "I, I wanted to make sure that the guy didn't come back to bother you."

"It's okay." Becky gave him a slight smile. "That was sweet of you."

Her reaction gave him enough confidence to continue with the real reason he returned. Danny dug into his pocket and revealed the dollar bill she had given him; it was crumbled into a ball. "There's a Three Stooges picture playing at the brand new movie place. I have enough for the two of us to see it." Danny bit his lower lip.

"Now, that's *really* sweet of you, but I'm going for a job interview over at the newspaper; it's right around the corner," Becky said. "Uhm, maybe some other time," she added.

Danny's eyes opened as wide as saucers. "You're gonna be a girl reporter, like Lois Lane?" His voice squeaked higher with every word.

There was a whole bunch of truths she could have uttered, but it was easier instead, to simply say, "That's the plan, kid."

# CHAPTER FOUR

Becky stood in front of a battered metal desk in the foyer of the Gazette's newspaper building. In a utility sized room located directly behind the desk was a middle-aged, balding man talking on the phone. Newspapers were stacked up high near one of the corners looking like they could tumble at any moment. With one hand the man held a black phone base with the receiver part seemingly glued onto his neck. Somehow he was managing to pace back and forth within the confines of the room.

As Becky continued to wait she glanced around at the walls. They were painted the ugliest shade of green she had ever seen. *They couldn't have picked this color on purpose. Okay, Becky, just get this over with to appease Mom.*

"No, I'm sorry the editor-in-chief is still not in. Yes, I'll be sure to tell him *everything* you said, verbatim."

Becky felt that the man's tone of voice was more than a tad condescending.

He shoved the receiver hard onto the base. Red circular marks lingered on his neck. He murmured a few words before stepping out into the foyer, putting the phone onto the desk.

"I hope you're not here trying to sell me something," he grumbled. "I have plenty of Tupperware from my first marriage."

"What did you get from your second marriage?" Becky tried to stop herself but it was too late, the words escaping from her mouth. "Oh God, I'm sorry! I can't believe I actually said that!"

"Nothing to be sorry about. It was heartburn my dear, lots and lots of heartburn," the man said as he loosened his dark blue tie.

Becky wondered roughly how many times this man was divorced. "I was kidding," she apologized.

"Well sweetheart, I wish I was." He retightened his tie. "So, if you're not here to sell me Tupperware why are you here? And do I detect a northern accent?"

Becky was impressed; even though her mom was born and raised in Jersey City, her father was from Georgia. Becky always thought of herself as having virtually no discernable accent. She gave the newspaper employee a half smile for his detection. "From New Jersey. I was here to see the chief editor…about a job as a reporter." She did not sound sure.

The nearly bald man glared at her. "Well, miss 'from New Jersey', you have exquisitely bright eyes," he said straight-out.

"Thanks?" Becky said. She lowered her head slightly and shook it. "Listen, it's just as well that the editor is not in. I was going to show him some stuff I've written. But it doesn't matter; I fully expected not to get the job. To tell you the truth, I don't think I would even take the job if it was offered to me. I'm really sorry I wasted your time and about that marriage comment." Becky paused. "I'm going back home tomorrow anyway." She voiced that fact more to herself than to him. Although, she still lacked sureness of where she belonged.

The balding man rubbed at his early five o'clock shadow. "Well, since you're here, can I take a look-see?"

Becky shrugged and handed over her memo pad. It took the man seconds to read what took her days to write.

He handed it back to her. "Can you make coffee? Because that's a must if I'm going to hire you as a junior reporter."

A puzzled look shot across her face.

"Oh, did I forget to mention I was the editor-in-chief?" he professed.

"But you told the guy on the phone—" was all Becky could think to retort.

"That weirdo calls at least twice a week about someone stealing his newspaper off of his porch, but he's not even a subscriber. If you ask me, the town is full of weirdos, me included. Anyway, do you want the job or not?"

"Yeah, you make it sound so tempting," she rolled her eyes. "Thanks, but no thanks. As I said, I'm going home."

"There's no place like home, huh?" He pointed in the direction of the front door. "Well, just the same, I'll make this simple, pretty eyes…if you show up at nine in the morning you've got the job. If not, well then, have a great life in Joisey." He tapped his lips with his fingers. "You know, I think one of my wives was from New Jersey. No wait, it was New Hampshire. Come to think of it there wasn't anything new at all about her at all."

# CHAPTER FIVE

Taking the indirect way back to her apartment—which meant staying along the main street and through the town's older, original, shopping area—was what Becky suspected she needed to do to focus her thoughts. Although some of her thoughts she wouldn't have minded being wiped away clean, even if it meant wiping a part of her away. *Starting with the part where I feel the emptiness because of him.*

Only, she soon realized the walk didn't work out that way. Instead, every brisk step she took seemed to bring about increased confusion in her mind.

*Why did he have to go and offer me the job.* Her pace slowed... *Is this what life will always be about? Nothing but heartaches and a series of hard choices laid before you. I hope not* ....to a crawl.

*It can't be.*

Becky stopped upon seeing her reflection through the front glass of an empty store. She still had all intentions of going home. After all, she missed her own room, missed her mom's chocolate chip pancakes on a Sunday morning after coming home from church, missed swinging on the swing set that took her dad nearly the whole summer—along with the more than occasional muttering under his breath—to build. Even missed her sister. When they were younger they would play the summer away together. Then...then they were no longer younger.

*Turn back the hands of time, isn't that what the song says? But you can't can you?*

Reflecting back through the smudges of the window pane she saw a smile forming on her face. *I'll show Mom; I can have patience.* By habit she rubbed her arms with her hands; it comforted her somehow.

A young man walking along the main street gave Becky a wolf whistle as he passed by. She turned in time to watch him. He was dressed in blue jeans and a white tee-shirt. A cigarette dangled from his mouth as he glanced her way with a cocky James Dean like smile. He walked away turning the corner and out of sight.

"Okay, childhood over," Becky said to herself and then let out a short laugh. She continued on at a more brisk pace crossing the side street.

The next block comprised of five shops open for business. The first store, John's Bargain Store, took nearly a third of the block with the other four squeezed in. As Becky peered inside the bargain store through one of the right hand side glass panes, she saw table-sized bins filled with various merchandise. The wooden bin closest to the front door had white socks matched with children's toys. What she didn't see, though, were a lot of customers; at best there were a handful mulling about.

Taped onto one of the left hand panes was a large hand written sign. It read:

**We will ALWAYS have the lowest prices on everything.**
**No need to hoof it to the mall.**
**John's Bargain Store, your best family experience.**
**Open till six for your convenience.**
**Closed on Sundays and holidays.**

*Hmmm.* Becky couldn't help but wonder if the cluster of new inside stores—that only opened about six months ago with more fanfare than a presidential election, marching band included—was already financially hurting John's Bargain Store.

And if there was really a John, he probably already knew that the future of shopping had arrived and it meant big trouble for his future. She also wondered if 'John' knew that the mall was open until 9pm...every day.

Becky continued her lengthy stroll walking past the butcher shop, briefly breathing in the odd mixed aroma of sawdust and raw meat. She went right past the dimly lit shoe repair shop. Passing the cute small malt shop Becky stopped dead in her tracks and slowly doubled back. Leaning against one of the stools inside the malt shop was a pair of wooden crutches. She was almost certain that sitting next to the crutches was the Mudhogs player she had seen on the baseball field. With a strong urge to find out, she clumsily opened the door and walked in.

# CHAPTER SIX

A housemaid, wearing a tight fitting, violet-blue uniform that revealed some of her ample cleavage, opened the door wide to the Sawyer mansion. She took a step sideways to let her employers in. "Welcome back home," was her mantra upon their arrival. Her eyes skimmed across Mrs. Barbara Sawyer's face not daring to let their eyes meet. It wasn't much of a household secret that there was no love lost between the two of them. "May I take your wrap, Missus?" she asked in a heavy Mexican accent.

"No, you *may* not," Mrs. Sawyer said, mimicking the housemaid's foreign enunciation, purposely brushing the maid as she walked past. "You think occasionally the 'so-called' help could manage to get out of the way!" Barbara said to her husband, exposing a hint of her own Bronx, New York heritage.

"Sorry…dearest," Mr. Sawyer said.

"Yeah, I'll bet," Mrs. Sawyer muttered under her breath, though purposely clear enough to be heard.

"May I take your hat?" The housemaid fixed her wide, smiling, brown eyes firmly onto Mr. Randel Sawyer.

Randel heard the excitement in her voice. He handed his Cowboy hat to her and as she took it from him her hand lingered on his an extra beat.

"Will that be all, Mr. Sawyer?"

"For now, Camila. But I might need some *coffee* later," Randel said.

Barbara continued to walk through the spacious, chandelier lit, black and white marbled foyer toward a wide staircase that led to the bedrooms upstairs. She did not need to turn around to see that her husband would have winked at the housemaid and that he would have received a mousey, flirty look in response. She wouldn't even have been shocked if their housemaid had already unclasped one or two more buttons on her so-called uniform. Barbara imagined grabbing a butcher's knife to end her husband's eye twitching at anything with a skirt. A rare smile came to her face as she took off her Italian high heeled shoes and climbed the carpeted stairs.

A few moments later Randel entered the master bedroom through the spacious, nearly floor to ceiling double mahogany doors. His young wife was already standing behind an Oriental privacy screen in the far corner, only her shoes were visible. He went over to his dresser to place his tie in the top drawer while keeping his sight on the Oriental screen through the dresser's mirror; these days he could only imagine the tan skin of the woman who stood behind it.

"You know, lil' darlin', there was a time you would undress in front of me," he said still looking through the mirror.

"There was a short time, *dear*, when you were faithful. And don't use the term little darling; it makes my skin crawl," Barbara flung the clothes she was wearing over the privacy screen, landing noiselessly onto the plush rug. "Tell your harlot I need these washed twice. No wonder the team is called the Mudhogs, it was disgustingly filthy on the baseball field. I wish you'd sell that damn team." She stepped out wearing a white silk housedress.

"Is that all you took from today? You do realize that two young men died," Randel said.

"Those two men who died? What were their full names, dear?" Barbara said, and waited a few seconds for an answer she expected wasn't coming. "That's what I thought; so don't you dare act so high and mighty."

"At least I act human…lil' darlin'," Randel taunted.

In a single motion Barbara picked up one of her shoes and flung it at him.

Randel easily ducked and watched as the heel struck the dresser mirror chipping it. "Hmmm, seven years bad luck," he said.

"Well, anything has to be better than this," she said. A coolness replaced her anger and she saw it affected him more than anything she had ever screamed in the past. Twisting the knife further she added one more thing. "I want a divorce…dear."

Ignoring her request completely, Randel went down the stairs and through the hall toward the housemaid's bedroom. He stopped short of knocking on Camila's door, briefly visualizing her dark, curvy body sprawled out on the bed with little or nothing on. Odds were she would have dosed herself with her Evening in Paris perfume. He detested the smell, but it was a small price to pay for what she offered.

Randel continued further down the hall and then entered the library. He went straight to the crystal decanter of Scotch whisky, pouring a short drink. He gulped it down thinking he was hard pressed to remember a time when he hadn't cheated on his wife. Not that he cared. Admittedly, he gave more thought to his baseball team than to her, even if it was always losing a shitload of money. *Ha*! he mused, *so does my acid-tongued wife*.

It suddenly dawned on him there was another thing he cared about, above all else—his public image. She would, no doubt, try dragging him down with a long, drawn out divorce. He gave himself a double shot this time, pouring it down his throat as fast as the first drink. And another one.

*I'm not going through a messy divorce. I can change her mind. If not...*Randel laughed inside...*I'll just kill her*. This last notion clung to him a few seconds even though he didn't mean it—exactly.

"Flowers," he muttered. "I'll start by getting her a few dozen roses," he said, slurring the last couple of words. *Now, where did Camila put the goddamn phone book?* Randel barely glanced around the room before picking up the library phone and dialing the operator to connect him to a florist. There were already voices speaking on the house line. He nearly said hello, instead, he silently pressed the receiver to his ear.

"—eed to do." A woman's voice spoke. Randel then heard his wife laughing in response to the woman. He had never heard his wife laugh like that before. It was disconcerting to his ears.

*"I'm being serious,"* the woman said. Randel didn't recognize who the other woman was. Besides even if he did know, there was too much static on the line.

*"You're being crazy,"* his wife said. Of course, her voice came in loud and squeaky.

*"Crazy is spending the last year and a half in jail,"* the woman said. *"Promise me, honey. I said, promise me."*

*"Yes, fine, I promise, no more mentioning divorce,"* his wife said. *"It's only...the thought of having to let him touch me..."*

It was evident to Randel by the ease of her voice that his wife wasn't worried in the least that he might walk in on her conversation. But of course not, she knew right what he would be doing, and who he would be doing it with. Randel's throat closed to the point that he felt the air might have been vacuumed from the room. He wanted to say something in response...anything. His whole body tightened. He remained still.

*"Close your eyes and pretend it's Rock Hudson if you have to. I'll take care of the rest. Obviously, I don't mind getting my hands dirty."* Through the static the other woman spoke in a sickly sweet, motherly tone.

There was a pause. For a second Randel was sure the Twilight Zone-like phone call had ended. It hadn't.

*"Then, I'd get it all?"* his wife finally said.

*"No, honey, 'we'd' get it all."*

The conversation ended with an unceremonious click. Randel stood with the phone still pressed against his ear. After a few moments the taunting short spurts of sound indicating the phone was off the hook started. He slowly put the phone receiver onto the cradle.

There was an urge to dive straight into the decanter of

liquor. Without taking another sip he left the library and rapped louder than he wanted to on the housemaid's door. She opened it quickly, standing there in a thick cotton robe that pooled to the ground. The sound of water running came from her bathroom.

Camila put her finger to her lips. "SHHHH. Do you want wife to hear? I thought you forget about me." She glided her finger over his lips.

"Where did you put the phone drect…di-rect-ory?" he said.

"What?" Camila said. She could see his cheeks were flushed. "Have you been drinking?"

Randel put his thumb and pointer finger together and then separated them somewhat.

"Well, Mr. Sawyer, I was about to take a bath. Care to join me?"

Randel gave a nod of his head figuring he would deal with what he overheard tomorrow when his mind was clearer. For right now, he didn't care to think about such things.

Camila let her robe hit the ground and proceeded to her bathroom. Shutting the water off she entered the tub; her breasts peeking temptingly over the bubbles. "Are you going to come?" she asked flirting and teasing.

## CHAPTER SEVEN

The town's only malt shop was the place to go for a first date for teenagers and the young at heart alike. The unwritten law of etiquette, at least in this town, was that on the second date you got to share a milk shake with two straws. Becky had had a blind date here—at Donna's strong urging—about six months ago. She never did get to the two straw stage, although, she did politely thank her friend for the introduction anyway. After that her heart was stolen and then broken in two because of another man.

A few steps inside the malt shop Becky stood frozen in place. She stared at the man sitting at the counter, his crutches leaning inches away.

*What am I doing?*

Behind the counter were oversized photos of ice-creams hanging crookedly on the wall by design. The pictures were the only thing staring back. She was trying to figure out her need to know if this was the baseball player she had seen earlier. Her need to know how he had been affected by the deaths of his teammates. Becky knew it was more than that.

The only other patrons in the place were two pregnant women sitting across from each other in a booth nearest a red and silver jukebox. Splish Splash had just finishing playing. Then a scratching sound started followed by Mack the Knife. *Someone likes Bobby Darin.* One of the women was rocking a baby stroller with one hand while the other hand was free to manage her bowl of ice cream. The child was crying out sleepily. The other woman was going on about something using her hands and arms to orchestrate her words...not quite to the beat of the music though, which was oddly disconcerting to Becky.

"You can have a seat anywhere, little lady. I'll bring you a menu in a jiffy," a slim, middle-aged man with eyeglasses and a stained white apron said. The malt shop's employee wiped the black speckled counter with a towel before placing a milk shake in front of the guy with the crutches.

Suddenly, Becky felt the urge to get the hell out. She proceeded to do that when a loud sneeze erupted from the man at the counter. The sleepy cries from the young child in the stroller turned into wailing screams. The mother stopped shoveling the ice cream into her mouth long enough to shoot a nasty look across the shop as she began rocking the stroller a little faster.

"God bless you," Becky automatically said.

The man with the crutches turned slowly around to face her. It was him, the Mudhogs' first baseman. His face blanked for a moment and then the end of his lips turned up slightly into a smile. "Thank you."

"You're welcome," she said, trying to keep the thin strand of conversation going. Becky was prepared to mention something about the weather next if nothing else came to mind.

The first baseman gestured to the empty seat next to him. Becky stood her ground for a second or two and then walked over to him, plopping herself down onto the round swivel stool. The thick black cushion made an odd squishing sound.

At close range she noticed he hadn't shaved in a day or three and his thick nut-brown hair needed a combing desperately. He looked tired, worn out. Still, she couldn't help but notice how ruggedly handsome he was, and she was getting more and more nervous by the heartbeat.

For the next awkward moment or two Becky's eyes drifted to those crooked pictures on the wall. She needed to tell him how sorry she was about the bus crash, about losing his friends. Ask how close he'd been to them. That she knew a bit about loss herself. That's why she was here, right? Becky swiveled her body, forcing herself to face the baseball player, to get it over with. "I—"

"What can I get ya!" the shop's employee said with extra enthusiasm as he loomed squarely in front of her.

Becky twitched from surprise and she shook her head. "Thanks, but I'm not staying."

"Just so you know, they make the best shakes in town," the first baseman said, putting in his two cents as he played with the straw stuck fast in the middle of his thick shake. "Not to sway you to stay or not." His voice sounded a little hoarse.

*I think they're the only shakes in town*, she mused. "Vanilla. Vanilla shake…please," she requested, giving the first baseman a sideways glance. "Maybe a little attempt at swaying?"

"Vanilla? Do me a flavor." It was apparently the shop's employee's standard rehearsed joke. "We have five whole other ice creams, pistachio being my favorite," he added and waited a few beats. "Okay then, vanilla it is. An oldie, but still good."

The two pregnant women with crying baby in tow gathered up all their belongings to leave.

"Have a nice day, ladies," the employee yelled out with barely a nod from them in return.

The one woman was still talking with her hands moving in the air saying something about her damn leaky pink fridge and going back to an ice-box. After they left the establishment, the shop was quiet.

"Well kids, it looks like you got the whole place to yourselves," the employee said and then disappeared through a swinging door that led to the hidden storage area.

When she turned her attention to the first baseman his hand was sticking out toward her. "I'm Joseph; friends call me Joey."

She took his hand and shook it quickly up and down once. "Becky, but you can call me...Becky." She covered her face for a second while shaking her head. "I'm sorry, can I retract that?"

Joseph smiled briefly. "It's okay to be nervous. Sometimes fans see me off the field and don't know exactly what to say."

Becky chuckled. "I'm sorry; I'm not really a fan. The most I know about baseball I got from Abbot and Costello's who's on first routine. Yesterday, I wouldn't even have known who you were."

"Oh," Joseph said. "But, weren't you by yourself in the

first row?"

"I was with a friend who's a fan. We, I, was really there paying my respects," she said.

Joseph nodded knowingly.

Becky took a quick sip of her milk shake. "This is pretty good." She took a longer sip.

"A…guy friend?"

Her face heated. "No…" she said, keeping her eyes focused on her milk shake, "…a friend who is a girl." Uncomfortable, Becky changed the direction of the conversation. "Uhmm, I was surprised to see you in here."

"I was hungry," Joseph said. "You know, ice-cream, the lunch of champions. Mostly, I needed to get away from everyone, clear my head."

"I'm sorry, I really should leave you alone then," she stammered.

"Actually, I'd rather have the company," Joseph said. "Please stay."

"Uhm, sure."

"So, not too hard to guess you weren't born here," Joseph said with his lips on his milk shake straw.

"I know, that's pretty apparent," Becky said. "I went to college here. I'm going home to New Jersey tomorrow."

"New Jersey? So if I asked you to join me next week for another milk shake…"

"It would have to be in New Jersey," Becky said. She added snidely, "Besides, how many girlfriends must you already have?"

"Well, Becky, between baseball and helping my parents on their farm whenever possible…zero girlfriends at the moment."

"Oh." Becky took a nervous sip. "Then that was sweet of you...but like I said, I'm going home tomorrow."

"That's too bad."

The employee returned with a new tub of ice-cream to put in the front freezer and then he began cleaning the back counter at the far end.

Becky reminded herself why she came into the store in the first place. "I'm really sorry about your friends. It must have been horrible going through what you and your team went through," she said. "Were you...very close to them?"

"No." Joseph's face turned angry as he averted his eyes from hers.

Uneasy, Becky stood. "Listen, I'm going to go now. It was nice meeting you, Joey."

"It should have been me, I should have died in that crash, not them," Joseph blurted.

As his words sunk in Becky gradually sat down, her face emptied. When she finally spoke, her voice quivered. "Why did you say that?"

Joseph stared straight ahead. "I wasn't with them. I wasn't on the bus. I wasn't on the damn bus."

"But the crutches?" Becky said.

He turned toward her, his eyes watery. "Yeah, right, the crutches," he scoffed, his voice unsteady. "I hurt myself tripping down a flight of stairs. How stupid right?" He pulled the straw out of the shake only to shove it right back in. "I wanted to go with the team anyway, but Mr. Sawyer, the owner of the team, wouldn't allow it. Was afraid I would hurt my leg even more."

"It's understandable, Joey, you're feeling guilty, but you know you didn't cause the accident, right?" Becky said.

"I know that," he said. "It's just I always—"

Joseph stopped talking as he and Becky heard several voices coming from right outside the shop. Both watched the employee dart from behind the counter holding a sign that said **Broken**. He hurriedly taped it onto the jukebox. Almost as soon as he was behind the counter again, a group of teenagers strutted in bringing with them thunderous laughter. All the boys had short, slick hair and the girls tight pony tails and cheerleading sweaters.

As they began to confiscate two of the booths, one of the boys yelled out to the shop's employee. "Hey, four eyes, when is the stupid jukebox ever gonna get fixed!" They continued to cackle.

The employee gave a sly grin to Becky and Joseph before going over to the school kids with an order pad and pen in hand.

Joseph proceeded in a lower tone. "I always sit in the front of the bus. Eddy and Rich always sat in the back. I wasn't there, so they sat in the front instead, and then..." He trailed off. "If Mr. Sawyer had only let me go with them."

Becky's face flushed and she slid from the chair. "It wasn't your fault," she said, and with Joseph watching her, she walked straight to the door. Her hand wrapped around the doorknob for a moment or two.

She turned her head and spoke over the teenagers laughing. "Joey, did you say next week for the other milk shake?"

"Yeah, cause I'm going to travel with the team for a few away games. I would have said Monday at noon. But New Jersey is a long way to travel for a milk shake, even a really good one," Joseph said, showing a hopeful smile.

Becky opened the door. "You know…I don't think I'm leaving just yet. I'll be here next Monday. I hope you will be too." She stepped outside where it was quiet. Once more she heard her heart beating out of her chest.

Inside the shop the employee wandered over to Joseph. "JT, do want another milk shake?"

The baseball player was still looking toward the front door. "Nah, I've had enough."

"She *was* cute; you should marry her one day," the employee joked.

"That's the game plan, Tommy," Joseph replied sincerely.

# CHAPTER EIGHT

Becky found herself standing inside the corner payphone once again. She paused a moment to catch her breath from her fast walking pace as she waited for her mom once again to answer the operator's request.

"Mom, I've decided to stay in Georgia for a while," she burst out as soon as she thought she heard her mother accept the call. When her mother asked why, Becky continued.

"Why? Well, Mom first of all the newspaper gave me a job if I wanted one. I can start tomorrow, and I'm going to…yeah, Mom, I think its good news too…I promise, Mom, I'll still call you nearly every day…I'll miss you too, but I…I really think I've found a reason to stay in Georgia. And mom, I'll show you, I do have patience…I know, I know you didn't mean it…I love you too."

Becky hung up the phone and stepped out into the fresh air with determination and a smile.

# CHAPTER NINE

Shielding her eyes from the sun, Fran Amaro followed the upwards path of her own hand stretching toward the sky until her sight reached the top of the tan bricked structure and to the metal cross that stood atop it. She thought it gleamed downwards like the spiritual sign it was meant to be, or in her case, perhaps, an ominous warning. Fran let a laugh escape at the latter notion.

Her smile lingered, because after eighteen months she did not have to breathe in the stale smell of her jail cell or the stench of her cellmate. And besides that, there was the unorthodox location her cousin had picked for their so-called family reunion.

Before walking up the concrete steps of the church Fran pulled down on her bright, floral print dress in an attempt to cover more of her legs. Her new look, which included red high-heeled shoes, felt utterly uncomfortable. Still, she'd rather die than ever willingly let anything oversized or dull, blue-grey cover her skin again.

Fran pulled open the heavy unlocked door and entered

the church. She had to let her eyes adjust to the dim lighting for a second before spotting her cousin sitting three pews in. For the few steps she had to walk down the aisle, her high heels clicked on the smooth stone church floor. Close to the altar were the only other people in the church—an elderly man and woman on their knees with their hands clasped together in prayer.

Before sitting down next to her cousin, Fran unconsciously began to make the sign of the cross; a habit instilled in her when she was a much younger version of herself; a habit she could have sworn broken the day she ran away from her nightmarish home. Before completing the shape of the cross Fran abruptly stopped her hand's motion.

The two women took a good long look at each other before Barbara Sawyer stood giving Fran a hug. "It's really good to see you," Barbara said, her voice nearly lost in the empty vast church. "I almost didn't recognize you, you're so…thin. Was it horrible?"

"Horrible?" Fran said. Even with only the one word said in return, Fran's Brooklynese came through loud and clear. "Honey, let's just say time moves along differently in prison."

"I can't believe you're really here. Thank God you got out unscathed," Barbara said as they both sat down in the pew.

"Not quite," Fran said. She pulled up her dress showing a two inch jagged scar higher up on her thigh. Barbara gasped as Fran continued. "The bitch used a mop bucket handle, who would have thought? In there, almost anything can be turned into a weapon. Ha, but she was only the first of a few lovely roommates. Honey, trust me,

I saw a lot of things I could tell you about, it could have been much, much worse."

The elderly man and woman stood up, exited the pew, genuflected, and then hobbled down the aisle, hand in hand, toward the church's exit. Both Barbara and Fran watched as the couple finally disappeared outside into the sunlight. As soon as the church door closed tight the cousins faced each other again.

"So we're sticking to my game plan?" Fran said. "Meet your husband, get close enough to get as much dirt as possible on the jerk for you to use against him. If we do this thing right you'll get much more than half of his estate."

Barbara grabbed a piece of paper from her purse. "This is the address of the hotel you'll be staying in. You're registered under the name, Susan Jones."

"Really? Susan Jones? Do I look or sound like a Jones to you?" Fran muttered as she studied her cousin's face. "Barb, game plan?"

Barbara ignored her cousin's question as she reached into her purse for a set of keys which she handed over to Fran. "This is to the blue sedan parked right in front of the church. You do remember how to drive, don't you?"

Fran pursed her lips. "Yeah, cute. Honey, I remember how to do a lot of things I've been aching to do."

"Speaking of that, on Tuesday and Wednesday nights, Randel goes to your hotel lounge for drinks. You're a bit older than his taste for women but wear what you're wearing now and after a few drinks you'll have him wrapped around your fingers." Barbara's eyes darted around, never making direct contact with Fran.

"Then, I guess, sex with him after he's had a few

drinks," Fran breathed heavily. The notion actually excited her for a moment.

"Well, Cuz, I'm afraid in that department you'll be disappointed; the whole thing should last three minutes tops," Barbara said bluntly.

"Three minutes is better than none, right?" Fran said. She waited for any kind of reaction from her cousin. She did not receive any. "One positive thing about being in jail, it has helped me read people better. So, what the hell are you not telling me?"

"Fine." Barbara peered at her cousin with her shark-like eyes. "I've added a slight wrinkle to the plan. I still want you to find out all you can." Her words were void of emotion. "Then—" Barbara slightly tilted her head.

"Oh my God, you want me to kill him?" Fran asked surprised but only somewhat shocked.

Barbara gave the slightest shrug. A moment of silence passed. "It may have crossed my mind."

"I've never killed anyone in cold blood," Fran finally voiced.

"Your boyfriend?"

"That was self-defense…mostly."

A creaky door opened and closed from somewhere behind the altar. Within a couple of seconds a priest appeared and he began re-arranging the candles on the marbled stoned altar table. He gave a nod to the two of them before exiting from where he came.

"It was a silly notion. Forget I said it," Barbara said.

Of course it was more than a notion, Fran knew that. She also knew enough her cousin wasn't going to let her forget it anytime soon. "If I—if *we* do this, we have to be very smart. First of all, after I leave this church we

47

wouldn't be able to contact each other for a long while. I'm not going back to jail. And you certainly don't want to end up there; trust me, not with a pretty face like yours."

A darkened smile crept onto Barbara's face. "Yes, smart and inventive. This is what I was thinking..." Barbara began.

# PART II

*1961 June*

NATIONAL NEWS
Top song by a female artist. I Fall To Pieces, by Patsy Cline

LOCAL NEWS
WOEFUL MUDHOGS LAND IN LAST PLACE—
The Farmstead Gazette

## CHAPTER TEN

The rented automobile was steered onto the grassy shoulder of the dirt road and then with a not so calm hand the car key was turned quieting the engine's humming. The silence made the driver's ears ring. Rolling the window down to bring in some outside noise, bring in some fresh air, didn't seem to help much. Nope, not much at all.

*So...testing one, two, three; testing one, two, three*, the driver thought glibly, knowing once the plan began, there was no going back.

*Relax*.

On the floor of the passenger side, nearly hidden in the farthest corner, was a crumpled piece of paper left there perhaps by the last renter. Curious, the driver picked it up and smoothed it. The handwriting on it only said, 'to my beautiful snow angel'. *Hmmm, did the snow angel know she was loved?* The unfinished note was crushed and flung back into the corner.

The driver grabbed a pair of sunglasses from the

passenger seat, and after straightening the hair on the top of the head, put them on. There was a hint of a smile when he didn't recognize the image in the rear view mirror.

*There were those in the world that made light of killing, of murder*, the driver supposed, while finally exiting the car. *Still, others probably had serious discussions about spearmint gum*. This last impromptu comparison nearly brought about a laugh.

Leaning against the car, the driver stared past the shoulder of the road at the vast farm fields, pondering exactly what kind of grains were being harvested there. The sunshine was bright and warm on the face. The fields seemed lit up in wondrous shades of gold. His face quickly turned solemn though, as the driver finally turned to see across the other side of the road...to a house standing alone...to where Bernie lived. Good old lovable Bernie—people have said.

The driver tried to take a normal breath in and out before heading toward the house at a slow, deliberate pace. *It felt a bit like walking the last mile*, the driver supposed. *Last chance, nothing is in stone, is it?* The thought suddenly exploded into the brain.

"But it's already literally written in stone, don't you think?" the driver whispered with a nervous laugh before continuing on the destined path.

## CHAPTER ELEVEN

The whistle started low, building to a relentless high pitch scream.

"For crying out loud, I'll be right there!" Bernie yelled toward the kitchen. He sat on the edge of his bed donning his neatly pressed blue shorts and white shirt. He almost forgot about leaving the flame on underneath the metal teapot and finished tying the one sneaker he had already slipped on before jumping up, leaving the other shoe laying on the floor. He felt around the mattress for his coke-bottle eyeglasses, then placed them on his face. *There, that's somewhat better*, Bernie thought.

Going into the kitchen, Bernie shut the flame off. As he reached for the teapot's handle, a rapping began outside his front door. Turning his head toward the sound, his fingers touched the hot metal surface instead. "Darn it...sugar!" Bernie shook his hand in the air as if somehow that would stop the burning pain that instantly started. "I'll be right there!"

The only people who ever knocked on his door were

the Jehovah's Witnesses. They always seemed to have a lot of patience with people, so he figured they could wait a moment or two longer. He moved quickly to the sink letting cold tap water run on his fingers for a few seconds as the rapping continued. The pain lessened a degree or two; the annoyance of the rapping did not.

"I said, I'll be right there!" he yelled. Excuses why he couldn't let them in or even talk to them at any length were already conjuring inside his head.

Bernie looked at his feet. One sneaker was on, the other still patiently waiting for him in his bedroom. "Oh, whatever," he muttered, and with only the one shoe he slightly limped his short body through the compact kitchen to the paint-chipped wooden door. He swung it opened and only a screen door separated him from his visitor.

Bernie expected to see at least two people holding books. There was only a single person standing on his nearly ground level porch—one he did not recognize through the mesh—and not a spiritual book in sight. What he saw was a smile on the person's face as the unexpected visitor was pointing somewhere across the way.

"I'm really sorry to bother you," the visitor spoke louder than necessary. "Is there any way I can use your phone? My car broke down."

Bernie angled himself and saw an automobile pulled off onto the side of the road. Dust from the road clung dearly onto the side of the car. "Oh…sure…of course." He slid up the tiny aluminum latch that was mostly holding the warped screen door shut against any strong winds that might come along. Although, at the moment, the air outside had become dead still.

"Watch your step. It goes up a few inches." Bernie side-stepped to let the person in and then by habit re-latched the screen door.

"Thank you so much," the visitor said. "This is very kind of you. I'm glad you were still at home. I don't know what I would have done if you weren't." The words rambled together.

"You're a bit off the beaten path," Bernie agreed. "It would have been at least a three mile walk to the main road."

"Then, I'm *very* glad that someone was home." The visitor glanced around the inside of the house. "This road does seem somewhat deserted."

"I like it like that. Were you going to visit Teddy?" Bernie said.

"Who?" the visitor thought to be prepared for any question that Bernie might have posed, but was completely caught off guard with this one.

"Teddy. He owns the farm across the way?" Bernie said, he could tell the person standing in his kitchen had no idea what he was talking about.

The visitor's head shook back and forth. "No, uhmm, actually, I'm a little lost. Actually, I'm a little embarrassed too; I might have ran out of gas. The stupid gas gauge stopped working the other day."

"Oh, well, those things happen. I hope you don't have one of those foreign cars. There's a reason they're so cheap, those things break left and right."

The visitor's head shook. "Chevy…Chevy Impala."

"Well anyway, nowadays Teddy tries to maintain the whole darn farm by himself. Poor guy, his wife passed on not more than a year ago," Bernie said, with a sad look on his face.

The visitor glimpsed through the screen door's mesh attempting to spot if there was any movement at all in the fields of the farm. "Really, so, do you see him...often?"

"As a matter of fact," Bernie said, "this would be around the time I would see him, if I see him at all. He likes to walk through the fields, inspecting his crops I guess."

The visitor looked one more time through the mesh without seeing anything or anyone. "I notice you're brewing tea, after I make my call could I impose on you for a cup before I go? It's pretty dusty out there."

Bernie smiled. "Of course, where are my manners?" He pointed to the phone hanging on the wall. "There's the phone. I'm going to finish getting ready to go to work, then I'll pour you some."

"Thanks, you're too kind. But I can pour us both tea while you're getting ready. Hey! Wait a second!" The visitor waggled a finger toward Bernie. "I recognize you, you're the guy who works at the baseball stadium, Bernie, right? I read about you in the newspaper."

Bernie blushed a little. "Yeah, that's me."

"Wow!" the visitor said. "A real celebrity in our midst."

Bernie's face became redder as a chuckle escaped him. "I'll be right back, okay?"

Pausing a second, the visitor picked up the phone but did not dial a number. "Hello...yes...thank you so much... I'll be waiting." And then rested the receiver onto the cradle. "Thanks again, help is on its way," the visitor yelled.

"You're welcome," Bernie said from inside his bedroom.

The visitor found two mugs easily enough, poured the tea quickly and reached toward a pants pocket.

Bernie came into the kitchen with a smile and both sneakers on.

The visitor's hand snapped up. "That was fast."

"I only had to put my other shoe on," Bernie said. "Thanks for pouring the tea."

With some quick thinking the visitor clasped one hand into the other. "Ow! I must have cut myself. Would you happen to have a Band-Aid?"

"Sure, I'll be right back." Bernie disappeared into the bedroom.

The visitor reached again for the pants pocket and pulled out a small vial of clear liquid. Quickly it was poured into one teacup and then the visitor picked up the other one. For a fleeting moment there was a notion to pour Bernie's cup down the drain and leave, get into the car and never stop driving.

The visitor remained still.

Bernie returned and handed off the Band-Aid, watching as the visitor put it on one of the fingers.

They both sat down and started sipping their tea. "I don't have company often," Bernie said. "Actually, not at all." He took two sips in a row. "It's a little bitter today, sorry about that."

"Is it? I hadn't noticed," the visitor said, taking another sip before gently placing the cup onto the table.

Bernie took a few fast, short sips. "It's hot in here, isn't it?" He placed the cup down harder than he intended to, nearly tipping it over. "What were we talking about?"

The visitor gave a seemingly genuine smile. "I'm sorry, you know, you really are a nice person. But it had to start somewhere, right?"

Bernie didn't understand the question; he didn't understand much of anything anymore. Still, by habit alone and with a crooked odd grin on his face, Bernie took another sip of the warm, bitter tea. This time the cup fell right out of his hand making its way off of the table. Oddly, it bounced twice on the floor like a rubber ball before breaking into a few jagged pieces with its third strike.

Bernie's eyes narrowed.

With a last gasp of breath his head hit the kitchen's white, speckled Formica table with an unheralded thump.

A slight sigh escaped the visitor's mouth. "Well, that worked faster than I figured it would." The visitor gestured a hand toward the limp body. "Bernie, I do feel sorry that you are dead; I really do. I only imagined I'd feel...more. You know what I mean."

Stretching across the table, the visitor lifted up Bernie's limp arm as high as it would go and then released it watching it plop down onto the table. "I guess you don't know, anymore, do you?"

The visitor gazed awhile at the limp body before getting up to leave. "Well, anyway, nothing personal. Necessary evil and all that."

Moments later, while sitting in the rented car, the visitor saw movement from the corner of the eye in one of the rows of the farm's crops.

Nearly hidden by the stalks of corn, about fifty yards away, a rather large, bearded man in overalls was waving.

*So, Teddy lives and breathes.*

In one fluid motion the visitor stepped on the clutch, turned the ignition on, and then off before releasing pressure from the clutch.

"Damn."

The visitor took a deep breath while getting out of car waving back. And with a disarming smile, headed toward the farmer.

CHAPTER TWELVE

Becky sat a few rows behind the first base dugout with her notebook and pen in her hands. The combination of a chilled breeze and the warm sun beating down on her face felt pleasurable, peaceful. She placed her writing materials on top of her purse which was resting on the slatted wooden chair next to her and closed her eyes wanting the peaceful feeling to go on as long as possible. With a slight smile on her face, Becky rubbed her arms up and down a few times until she was as relaxed as she was going to be.

Mentally she transported herself away from the stadium filled with strangers all around, to a secluded warm, pure white sandy beach. Suddenly, a man's familiar voice snapped her illusion away, whispering near her ear. "I am enamored with you, young lady."

Becky kept her eyes closed, and with her best poker face asked, "Is that you, Charles?"

"Hey, who the heck is Charles?" Joseph said much louder. In full player's uniform except for the baseball cleats, he plopped himself down on the empty chair next to her. He was grinning. "Aren't you impressed that I knew the word enamored?"

Becky gave him a quick kiss on his lips. "I'm impressed with everything you do."

"Even my .230 batting average?" Joseph said.

"Well, look on the bright side; it can only get higher, right? And your leg doesn't hurt you at all anymore," Becky said. "It doesn't hurt you anymore, right?"

Joseph shook his head. "I don't know, physically I'm fine, yeah, but…I still can't seem to find my swing after I got hurt. I'm sorry, Becky, that I keep repeating myself…about that. Anyway, how about after the game, dinner, a movie and we could go back to my place. I promise absolutely no talking about baseball or any other sport for that matter," he asked hopefully.

"How about dinner, a movie and then you walk me home," Becky countered. "And you can talk as much about baseball as you'd like."

"But we can be alone at my place," Joseph said.

"I know. That's what I'm afraid of," Becky said with a smile. "I don't trust us alone and you know I want to wait." She looked around the stadium. "Hey, Joey, this is the second day in a row with no Bernie passing out peanuts. Seriously, you think he's okay? They said last year he never missed even one game, this will be three in row. Has anyone heard from him at all?"

"I know, he's always here, I haven't heard anybody say anything," Joseph said. "Probably he came down with the flu or something. If I see the stadium manager, I'll ask." He suddenly looked straight ahead and talked through the side of his mouth. "Don't look now but that *woman* is heading this way." Becky turned her head slightly to see. "I said don't look," he repeated.

"Oh, Miss Barbara," she said in a low voice.

Joseph attempted to stand but Becky firmly placed her hand on his arm. "Don't you dare leave," she half-teased.

The eighty-two year old woman with gobs of makeup painted on her face and a too short, bright orange sundress made her way across the row of wooden seats to them.

Barbara didn't hesitate at all picking up Becky's things placing them one seat further away before sitting down next to her.

Again Joseph tried to stand to leave and stopped midway after witnessing Becky's hard glance.

"Isn't the weather simply dear today. I'm so glad, I could not have waited another day to wear my new sundress," Barbara said, her s's sounding more like a snake through her dentures.

"And aren't you two just the cutest things?" Barbara said way too sweetly.

"Hey, isn't that my manager waving me to come!" Joseph pointed toward the field. He stood completely and gave Becky a very quick kiss. "Sorry," he whispered.

"You should be," Becky whispered in return. "I was seriously thinking of going over to your place tonight."

"No, you weren't," Joseph spoke a little louder than a whisper. "Were you?"

"You'll never know now sweetheart, will you."

"Joseph, I've been meaning to tell you," Barbara said, "we should stop looking for curve balls. Cause they're throwing the fastball right by us. And we should try to keep our eye on the ball more when we swing. We need a few more wins under our belt."

"Yes, Miss Barbara, I didn't think of that. We should look at the ball more." His sarcasm was wasted on her. "See you after the game Becky, and have a nice day," he added looking directly at Barbara. He then quickly jogged away.

"He's a keeper," Barbara said. "Rebecca, dear, I read your little story about Farmer Teddy, very nice."

"I prefer Becky."

"No, I think Rebecca is more elegant. Anyway, dear, I was wondering if you'd like to do a story on me."

"About?"

"Well, Rebecca, basically the same thing, you could do a story on my gardening. I have just the loveliest garden you'll ever see." Barbara smiled broadly, looking a bit like a clown with her makeup.

"I'll be sure to bring it to the attention of the chief editor," Becky said in her own overly sweet voice.

Barbara stood up futilely pulling down on her sundress. "That's all I ask. You are a dear. I'll be waiting to hear from you."

Becky watched her walk away and then closed her eyes again in search of the beach daydream once more.

## CHAPTER THIRTEEN

Once more Fran detached her prison thin, nude body from Randel's. She didn't care that it was only two in the afternoon and that she was already getting more than a bit...sore. She did not care one iota.

"Damn," was the only word that Fran could muster to say, as she gazed toward the vaulted ceiling.

"You said that the last two times," Randel said.

"Did I?" Fran said. "Yeah I guess I did." Her words had a sleepy overtone to them. Drowsiness was overtaking her. But this was the first time Randel Sawyer had invited her over to his home and who knew if she would ever get this golden opportunity again. She had to stay awake, wait for *him* to fall sleep and then search the house for something, anything her cousin could use against him. But she was so very sleepy from the combination of sex and wine, and more sex, and more sex. It didn't help her cause any that he was speaking to her in such a soft, monotone voice. Soft, she thought to herself which was so ironic since he was so—

"Susan, you seem so surprised that it felt so good," Randel said.

*Susan? Oh right my damn name is Susan...what a stupid name. I wish he'd stop talking so softly.*

Fran smiled at him, at least she attempted to. Her lips were feeling kind of numb at the moment. *Well, your wife told me you were piss poor in the sack, honey. But I'm sure glad I didn't kill you right off like she wanted me to. I can always kill you any time, sex like this doesn't come around too often, if ever.* "Well, you hear stories of older guys losing their stamina in bed," she finally said.

"And, with me?" Randel spoke smugly.

"I think you know," Fran stated.

"I want to hear it. Tell me I'm your best," Randel said.

"You *are* the best," Fran replied. It was the first truthful thing she had said to him since she purposely spilled some of her drink on herself after literally bumping into him in the hotel's lounge. Then she stood there and let him meticulously dry her dress off everywhere. She even guided his hand some.

Randel smirked, reached over to the night table, and poured the last of the red wine into her glass nearly filling it. With the glass in his hand rolled his body over to face her. "Here, have more wine."

Fran knew she should not indulge in even another single drop but grabbed the wine from him anyway nearly drinking half the glass in one gulp. He was staring at her. "What? You made me thirsty!"

Randel smiled. "I was only thinking how beautiful you are."

Fran didn't know if it was the wine or not, but his words made her feel warm, terribly warm. Her eyelids were shutting on her and she was losing the will to fight it. Fran pointed feebly at a painting hanging on the closest wall to her. "What is that supposed to be?"

"That my dear, is an original signed Picasso," Randel said, with a smug look cemented on his face.

"No slit, ha…I mean, no shit," Fran stammered as she almost dropped her glass onto the bed. "Do you really like it?"

Randel took the glass from her shaky grip placing it back onto the table. "Not really, a six year old could do better. I like it's a signed Picasso, though." He spoke his words in his softest tone yet. She was falling asleep.

"A Picao, hanging in a guest ro-" Fran's eyes shut tight with her mouth slightly open. Seconds later she started to snore rhythmically.

"It has to hang somewhere, dear," Randel said to his sleeping guest as he got out of bed. Still naked he walked over to her purse and began searching through the contents until he came across a scrap piece of paper with writing on it.

Minutes later, fully dressed, he made a phone call. "I want you to drop whatever you are doing and get over here. Yes now! There's a woman here with me. Right Sherlock, it's not my wife. I need to find out why she has my private phone number written down on a piece of paper. Because *I* didn't give it to her! No…no strong-arming!"

Randel glanced at the sleeping naked body lying on his bed. "Don't worry, she can't hear me. I said…she can't hear me! With the amount of sleeping pills I put in her wine she won't be hearing anything for quite a while. Just get over here take her picture. See if you can find anyone who knows who she is."

Twenty minutes later Randel let the detective in. The stocky private eye stumbled in wearing a twenty dollar gray suit with a red shirt and a Polaroid land camera strung awkwardly around his neck. "You know, your team is losing again," the private detective said.

"What else is new. The team is the least of my concerns at the moment," Randel said, glaring as he pointed toward the bed. "That's her."

"Holy crap! She's naked!" the detective yelled. He squeaked, as if he had just sucked in a balloon full of helium.

"Yeah, can't slip anything past you, huh detective. Now find out who the hell she is," Randel ordered. "Think you can do that?"

The detective took a couple of shots of her face and then turned to Randel. "Uhm, do you think you'd mind if I took a few for my, uhm, files."

"Knock yourself out," Randel muttered.

The detective finished taking other pictures of her from various angles, and then he went to the front door. "Mr. Sawyer, I'll pass them around see if anybody knows anything."

Randel handed the detective two crisp one hundred dollar bills. "Make sure you're here by morning. I want you to follow her around. I need to know everywhere she goes, everyone she sees. Got it?"

The detective snatched the bills from his hand shoving them straight into the pocket of his cheap suit. "Got it."

Randel locked the door behind him. A moment later

he was shaking his head; he could hear her trucker-like snores from across the room.

## CHAPTER FOURTEEN

With two outs in the last inning, every base had a player standing on it as Joseph made his way to home plate stopping a few feet short of the right-hander's batter's box. While taking a couple of practice swings he noticed that not a lot of fans had bothered to stay to see the last out. Four runs down and too many losses this year for them to believe there would be a different outcome.

He looked down at the handle of the Adirondack bat; he no longer felt at ease gripping it. Funny how when you're hitting well the bat felt like an extension of your arm, and now…

…He looked up into the stands for her and his mind drifted for a second to the beautiful ring he had stared at through the jewelry store's front window.

*And who could blame them.* Joseph thoughts turned back to the scarce crowd. *Our team is stinking up the place; I'm stinking up the place.* He now found himself in the precarious position of representing the tying run. In the past he would have found a way to get the ball over the fence. In the past he would have been the hero. A sarcastic laugh escaped him—*in the past my team would never be down by four runs.*

Joseph noticed that Becky had wandered down to the first row. He was tempted to give her a wave but knowing his volatile manager was watching from the top step of the dugout he looked away. Instead, Joseph picked up some dirt, rubbed his hands and handle of the bat with it and took one more practice swing. *Nope, a whole bucket full of dirt couldn't bring his batting average up*, he mused.

An image of the ring flashed into his head. A sterling silver double heart ring with a diamond placed in each heart seemed perfect for her. *She* was perfect, the most beautiful woman he had ever laid his eyes on. And he loved her with all his heart.

*Okay...okay...don't think about anything else but the ball coming out of the pitcher's hand. You can do this*, Joseph tried his best to spur himself on, *one good swing and this game is tied.*

All three players on base were clapping and yelling out encouragement, although no sincerity could be heard in their voices. He glanced at the dugout to see his manager, arms crossed over his chest, standing silent. The manager had the appearance of a man who had seen too many games go south on him.

Joseph looked up at Becky and *she* waved.

He gave her the subtlest of nods and then stepped into the batter's box. *Don't look for a curve ball*, the annoying woman's voice invaded his head. The right-handed pitcher wound up and released a fastball right down the middle of the plate. Joseph swung and the crack of the ball hitting the bat echoed throughout the nearly empty stadium. The baseball sailed up high and long but was foul by more than forty feet. Any fans who were left in the stadium were now on their feet.

The visitor's catcher leaped up from his crouched position and ran out to talk to his pitcher while Joseph grabbed some more dirt from the ground. His heart was pounding fast; he hadn't hit a round ball that *squarely* in a long time, maybe never, this whole dreadful season.

The ring he was going to finally have the nerve to buy tried to push its way back into his thoughts. *Don't think about anything.*

The catcher was already squatting behind home plate as the pitcher stood a second or two longer this time before letting another fastball fly out of his hand.

Joseph was ready for it. His swing connected once again. The ball flew high and far sailing seemingly mere inches on the wrong side of the foul pole. It bounced around the upper deck before plopping onto the outfield grass with a silent impact.

The visiting team's manager did his best impression of a jog as he went out to his pitcher. He seemed to be chewing tobacco and the pitcher out at the same time before slapping him hard on the back and returning to the dugout.

Joseph stayed in the batter's box staring straight at the pitcher. *A curve ball is coming. There's no way the manager is going to let him throw me another fastball. No way.*

He stood motionless as a ninety mile an hour fast ball screamed across the heart of the plate. "Strike three, you're out!" the umpire yelled. Joseph watched as the catcher ran out to the pitcher to congratulate him. He watched his manager disappear down the steps and through the dugout along with the rest of his teammates.

Not one person even glanced his way, except her. Becky was cutely shrugging and smiling at him. All he wanted was to hold her and tell her he was sorry he lost the game, and how he felt about her. At that very moment he realized that the game of baseball wasn't the most important thing in his life…she was.

Tomorrow he would buy the ring. In a few days during dinner at the fancy steak restaurant he would pop the question. When she said yes he would be the happiest man ever born.

He waved at her.

## CHAPTER FIFTEEN

A mingling of unpleasant odors coming from the locker room had made permanent residence in the narrow concrete hallway. Every time Becky went down there she did her best to ignore the smell. Every time she reminded herself never to go down to the locker area again.

The locker room door slammed open toward Becky. She took a couple of quick steps backwards nearly losing her balance as she tripped over her own size five feet. She let out a short high-pitched laugh at her own clumsiness. Becky was surprised at how good of a mood she was in. Things in her life were finally going well, really well.

"Good afternoon, ma'am," a tall baseball player said as he hustled past her and down the hallway which led to the player's dirt-covered parking lot.

"Afternoon, Slim," Becky greeted, although she was sure he was already out of ear shot.

The next player came out just as fast. "Ma'am."

"Big D," Becky said. "Sorry about the game."

"No big deal, we're kinda used to losing," he said deeply and kept walking.

And another. "Hey there Becky, JT is still in there," the player said.

"Thanks, Bob. They ran out of nicknames did they?" Becky quipped.

"What?" he said nervously moving his head up and down.

"Never mind, is everyone decent?" Becky said.

"Uhm, well, I don't know about decent, ha! But whoever is left is all dressed. A cop is in there too," Bob stated and went along on his way.

"Cop?" Her smile disappeared.

Only Joseph, the manager, and a police officer remained when Becky stepped into the locker room. The manager limped slightly as he headed to an adjacent room on the other side of the locker room and the police officer seemed to be walking straight toward her. Becky forced a smile.

"Officer, do you...can I help you?" Becky asked. The cop was now a couple of feet from her.

The officer pointed to the door Becky was standing directly in front of. "I need to get by you, ma'am."

"Oh, right, yeah. Have a nice day, Officer," Becky said and went right over to Joseph. She gave a very quick peck on his lips. After she did so she glanced back and watched the officer leave the room. "So, what gives; did someone call the cops because the team is going bad," she joked. He didn't crack a smile. She couldn't remember ever seeing him so serious.

Joseph pointed toward the door. "That was Marty; he's been a fan of the team for a long time. He recently became a police officer and he was making a courtesy call." He paused, and then sighed. "Yeah…so…they…they found Bernie. I'm sorry, Becky; he died—they're thinking a heart attack."

"What? No! He wasn't sick at all," Becky said. "I just interviewed him." She shook her head a couple of times. "That was stupid, I know you don't have to be sick to have a heart attack…but, this doesn't feel right to me!"

"I'm really sorry." Joseph shrugged. "I'm gonna miss the guy."

Becky shook her head again. "No! I want to go there."

Joseph had turned to close his locker tight. "Go where?"

Her voice went up an octave with every word she spoke. "To his house, to look around."

Joseph looked surprised. "Are you crazy, no way! There would be nothing to see. Besides you know you're not a detective right?"

Becky took a step backward. "First of all, I'm not asking for your approval, I'm going with or without you. And I do want to be an investigative reporter one day."

The two of them stared at each other.

The sound of a door opening and closing broke the awkward silence and the manager walked passed them on the way out. "You kids all right," he said gruffly; a lit cigar was dangling from his hand.

"Yeah, just great, Skipper," Joseph said with his eyes still focused on Becky.

"Peachy keen," Becky chimed in.

The manager paused to draw on his cigar, "Well, you kids have a good night then." As he reached the door to leave he turned to face them. "Try not to kill each other.

You're supposed to be in love, remember?" The manager opened the door and left.

"I do love you, you know." Joseph said sincerely.

"I know, me too," Becky said.

They hugged each other. "Joey, it's…it's something Bernie said to me after the interview. I didn't think that much of it at the time. He was saying that he had been having some strange dreams about someone following him."

"Dreams?" Joseph said.

"I know. I know it sounds silly. But maybe someone was really following him. I don't know. It's so strange he told me about it and now he's dead." Becky rubbed her arms. "I never did like coincidences. But, *sweetheart*, if you *really* don't think I should go…then…I guess—"

"No, we will go. I'll take you first thing in the morning. We'll look around, not find anything and that will be the end of that. Okay?" Joseph said.

Becky darted to him giving another quick kiss on his lips. "Yes! First thing in the morning. Thank you!"

## CHAPTER SIXTEEN

It took the usual couple of hours for Becky to succumb to the night. She valiantly kept her eyes open for as long as she was able. But even with the lights on and her body propped up against her uncomfortable pillows, sleep always came, as did her dreams...

Her sister was cowered in the corner in a fetal position her hands covering as much of her face as she could. In her dream she was curious why her sister would even be here, after all, she wanted nothing to do with her anymore, right? Her mom had blatantly said as much. Hadn't she? As hard as Becky tried she could not clearly see what her sister was attempting to hide with her hands. Her uncooperating legs wouldn't take her any closer. Becky went to flip the light switch on to take a closer look.

"No, Rebecca, keep the lights off." The voice, his voice, made her feel so safe, made her forget all about her sister. She could smell where he was standing in her room. She loved the smell of him. She had come to love everything about him.

"Come over here, baby." His voice again. It made her do anything it commanded. Keeping her arms stretched outwards Becky stepped carefully over to him, toward his words. She stopped inches short of his body, putting her arms down to her sides. Knowing what was coming next, she stood as still as possible waiting for him to start. Her chest began moving in unison with her heavier breaths.

He grabbed her sweater slowly pulling it off of her while brushing his hands against her. Becky could feel the wanting to be in his arms, the need to be in his arms. She desperately desired so much more than that from him. "I have to have patience." Her whispered words cut through the darkness. "I want to wait until we can marry." Becky longed to see his face, but it was becoming lost within vague shadows of her memories of him.

Suddenly, his lips touched hers. It felt electric and she lost complete control of her mind and body.

Later, they lay in bed as she held on to his body as tightly as she could. Because Becky somehow knew this was only a dream, yet she held on just the same, fighting as hard not to wake up as she had not to fall asleep.

His voice, his smell, her desires, all faded like a puff of smoke carried away by an unseen wind.

"Don't you dare leave me," she whispered. "I love you, even if you didn't love me." But the dream had ended, her eyes opened. He was gone as was her sister in the corner.

"He never really was with me, was he?" Becky's emptiness settled back inside of her as a teardrop made its way down her cheek.

It truly surprised her that there could be any tears left. *Apparently*, Becky sighed, *I'll never fully run out of them.*

CHAPTER SEVENTEEN

By the appearance of the nearly ominous darkened skies, Becky could have easily believed it was 7 o'clock at night instead of what it really was, 7 o'clock in the morning. The Georgia weather was being unkind. The heavy air could not have been any wetter without rain actually falling from the heavens. Even though she was standing still she already felt hot and sticky because of it.

She stayed on the small front stoop of her apartment dwelling waiting for Joseph to pull up in his red Chevrolet pickup truck. Becky wore baby blue shorts and a red plaid shirt; Joseph's favorite outfit. She was trying to keep him happy. *In all ways but the one way he probably wants the most,* she thought. Well, she had gone down that path before... not again, not ever again.

*Beep! Beep*! Joseph's truck's horn pried her from her thoughts and she dashed over to the truck, hopping inside with a big smile. "Good morning, Joey!"

"Hey, good morning, Becky. Did you sleep well?" he said. With his foot on the brake he put the truck in gear.

The vehicle didn't approve and made a grinding sound. He too was wearing shorts and a tank top that showcased his muscular arms usually hidden beneath the loose fitting baseball uniform.

"Like a baby," she said as she rested both her feet on his dashboard.

The truck groaned some more as if the engine needed to either cut out or jump forward. But Joseph hesitated taking his foot off of the brake. "Are you sure you want to do this? We're not gonna find anything, you know." He looked toward the sky. "And we'll probably get drenched for our troubles."

Becky leaned over and kissed his cheek. "Pleeease. Besides getting wet in this hot sticky weather sounds nice just about now."

"I had to ask," he said, shrugging and then released the brake. The truck lurched forward with yet a different clanking sound. "Yeah, I gotta get that fixed one day."

In a few minutes he was turning off the main road and onto the dirt road Bernie's house was on. He pulled over in front of the house and they immediately got out of the truck. The winds had started to swirl the dirt and straw around into small circles of debris. Not too far in the distance lighting began to skip and flicker about the sky.

Joseph grabbed Becky's hand as they walked closer to the house. "Man," Joseph said, "it's going to rain like crazy."

Becky started to pull him along. "Come on, then let's get inside before it starts."

They stepped onto the front porch feeling slightly safer if the rain were to start.

"I really don't feel comfortable breaking into his

house. It seems disrespectful in so many ways," Joseph said, while glancing around to see if anyone else was watching their foolish attempt of breaking and entering into a dead man's house. *If anyone even knew he died.* He hated that thought entered his head. But except for the dancing hay in the road the area was eerily deserted.

As Becky's hand grasped onto the front door's handle, the sky flashed a brilliant bluish gray for an instant. A deafening clap of thunder soon followed.

"See, Becky, even God doesn't want us going in."

She grabbed the handle and pushed the door open. "Or God unlocked it for us."

Becky stepped inside and into the kitchen. The lights were still on. Pieces of broken ceramic were scattered along the floor. Joseph tripped into the kitchen.

"It doesn't look like any of his family members, or… anybody, was here to clean anything up," Becky said. She looked closely at the floor where the biggest piece of porcelain lay; there was a brownish stain right next to it. She tapped Joseph on his arm and pointed downward toward the stain. Without uttering a word to him, Becky bent down putting her face as close as she could to it.

"Okay, what the heck are you doing?" Joseph said. More lighting flashed through the small kitchen window. This time it took a few seconds for the thunder to roar. The lights went off, came back on, and then finally stayed off.

"Becky, I really think we should go." He went to grab her hand fully expecting her to strongly argue her case as to why they should continue on.

"Okay," she said and put her hand in his.

They went outside staying huddled underneath the

small covered porch. The rain had started in full force. Porch roof or not, the raindrops, guided by gusty winds, were already getting them wet.

Within the mere seconds it took them to run to the truck they were both utterly drenched.

Joseph started the truck up right away. "I'm so sorry Becky. There wouldn't have been anything to find anyway."

She was staring out the window toward the fields of crops across the way. "Joey, it wasn't a heart attack."

"Sweetheart, you need to let this go. We all liked him but—"

"It wasn't a heart attack. He was poisoned. Someone did this to him."

"What?"

Becky faced him, as she sat uncomfortably in the truck with wet clothes that stuck to her like glue. She shivered, and she rubbed her arms to warm them. "In Biology one of the things I learned was what poisons smelled like. I figured it was a good idea in case I ever wanted to pursue a nursing career. To know what a patient may have ingested simply by using the sense of smell. I actually got a one hundred on that test. Anyway, I smelled the distinct scent of bitter almonds in the stain. That's what cyanide smells like. Someone put cyanide in his drink. We need to go the Farmstead Police Station."

"Come on Becky, really? You got that from smelling an old stain on the floor that who knows how long was there?" Joseph again tried to hold her hand. "Sweetheart, I—"

She jerked her hand up in frustration. "Don't! I know I'm right. It's not some kind of wild imagination or wishful thinking or whatever else might be going on inside your head, Joseph." She hesitated. "All right." She pointed toward the farm. "Let's see if Teddy saw anything."

"Teddy, who?" The truck's defrost was barely keeping up with the moisture that was forming on the windshield. Joseph tried looking through the windshield that was quickly fogging up inside from the storm raging outside.

"Teddy. He's the one who owns the farm right over there. I actually interviewed him recently. If someone came around here who didn't belong I would bet anything he saw...something," Becky said. She rubbed her arms again.

"Okay, fine. But...what if he didn't see anything?" Joseph said.

"Then...then I promise to you I'll drop the whole thing, honest," Becky said. "I'm not crazy," she almost whispered those last three words.

Joseph tried to smile. "Of course you're not crazy. But I do think you're letting your imagination get the better of you." He paused a moment. "Let's go see this Teddy fella." Joseph reached under his seat and grabbed a dirty rag, using it to help with the foggy windshield. It wasn't much better, but at least he could see enough to drive.

---

Becky told him to follow the crops along the highway, and then suddenly a grassy, uneven road would appear that led directly to the farmhouse. She explained the farmhouse was hidden from the main road by the taller crops. Joseph slowly guided the truck along the more muddy than grassy terrain. Soon the so-called road came to an abrupt end blocked by even more crops. There was a somewhat visible walkway that winded its way through the crops and presumably to the living quarters. Joseph wondered how Teddy got his tractor, or truck, or whatever farmers drove around town, onto the road.

Joseph moved to get out of the truck. "Wait!" Becky said. "Teddy is very skittish with strangers. I'll go up there and talk to him. You stay here." She put her hand on the door handle. "Anyway, no sense us both getting more soaked, right?"

"Are you sure?" he said.

She gave him a slight smile. "It's okay, really. I won't even go inside the house. Promise."

"No!" he said. "I'll follow close behind. I'll stay just out of sight at the edge of the crops." He wasn't going to hear any argument from her and started to step out into the bad weather.

"Fine." Becky took her shoes off leaving them on the floor of the truck. "I don't think these will help me much. Do you?" She left the truck, slamming the door behind her.

Joseph glanced down at his own shoes which were already a muddy mess.

Becky weaved her way through the makeshift walkway with Joseph a step or two in tail. As promised he stopped a few feet from the clearing watching Becky head to the farmhouse which was now in view about a couple of hundred feet away from them. The house was really a log cabin, modest in size. In the far corner of the house-length porch was a swing being silently pushed by the wind.

Reaching the house, she slowly climbed the porch steps. Lighting flashed across the sky. She paused for a moment then continued. Joseph watched her knock a few times on what he guessed was the front door. She turned to him and shrugged. Joseph waved for her to return. Becky raised her pointer finger toward him and moved to her right, tilting her head toward the house.

It seemed to him as if she was trying to look through a window. Although from Joseph's vantage point he could see no light coming from inside the house. He saw Becky cupping her hands to her face. Enough raindrops fell into his eyes to blur his vision. He wiped at his face with the back of his hand, once, twice, three times before being able to see well enough again.

Joseph heard something. He couldn't make it out exactly at first. Why would he, it wasn't a sound he expected to hear on this early stormy morning, and on a farm of all places. To top it off, in the middle of Farmstead, perhaps the most uneventful place on the whole planet. He connected the dots when he saw Becky oddly jumping as she pointed toward the house. It was screams he was hearing, Becky's screams.

Joseph slipped on the muddy grass causing him to slam into the muck. "Damn!"

He scrambled his mud-riddled body back up, with only his pride being hurt.

Her screams became louder, more unnerving. He darted to the house nearly falling up the stairs.

Becky's screams had actually been two words repeatedly screeched together. "In there! In there! In there!" He moved past her to a window that had a curtain hung askew. There was just the right amount of outside light to see through the window pane; to see deep within the room.

"Oh my God," Joseph said. With his muddy body he grabbed Becky and held her tight. "Don't look anymore." He guided her off the porch, through the walkway, back to his vehicle.

Once inside the truck, they couldn't seem to acknowledge each other. Instead, in silence, their sights remained straight ahead.

"Who would do that?" Joseph finally uttered with a shaky voice. He felt oddly cold, yet it had nothing to do with him being drenched beyond belief. He looked at Becky. She sat motionless.

"Are you okay?" he asked concerned.

She didn't answer.

"Sweetheart, are you okay?" His words came out louder this time. Louder than he intended. She nodded quickly.

"I told you. Someone poisoned Bernie...then..." She didn't finish that particular thought. "Oh my God, I interviewed *him* too."

There was some clearing in the fast-moving Georgia storm although the rain had yet to let up. Like long fingers, thin bands of sunrays surreally crept across the field making their way up to and over the crops to the roof of the farmhouse.

"The weather changes fast here, doesn't it," Becky said flatly.

Joseph nodded his head. "Yes it does." He paused a beat. "Are we actually talking about the weather right now?"

"Joey, I can't talk about what's inside that house yet," Becky stated.

"Who would do that?" Joseph repeated, trying his best to free the image stuck in his mind of the axe coming out from the back of the farmer's neck.

CHAPTER EIGHTEEN

Sitting in his two door Desoto, the detective had one bloodshot eye on the mom and pop grocery store that he had heard served decent enough eggs—*At least they didn't murder ya*, the guy had told the detective. His other eye was on his Timex wind up wrist watch. It was five after seven. The handwritten sign said it opened every day at seven. Mom and Pop lied.

He drummed his fingers impatiently against the dashboard in a silent beat. He had to get going soon. He knew Mr. Sawyer would surely kill him if he wasn't there to follow that naked girl. Well, she presumably wouldn't be naked anymore when he was following her. But the idea of that possibility made him grin for a moment.

The detective also knew he was starving, his oversized stomach told him that loud and clear numerous times in the last half hour or so. And there was the matter of his wife; he hadn't gone home at all, nor had he called her. If he had a coin in his pocket he might have stopped at a payphone—might have. He really didn't want to think what his life would be like the next few days at home. A living hell came to mind.

All night he had shown the naked girl's Polaroid head-shot around all the dives in town, with no luck. He wondered if Mr. Sawyer would have been surprised or not at how many places like that there actually were.

The lights finally came on in the store. It was at least five more minutes before the sign on the glass front door was flipped from closed to open. His watch said nearly seven thirty. He stepped out of the Desoto, took his jacket off, and tossed it onto the back seat of his car.

A bell that was tied to the front door barely clinked when he entered the mom and pop establishment. "Hey, I'm in a bit of a rush!" the detective said to the older woman standing motionless behind the counter. "If you could whip me up some eggs pronto, that would be just great." There was more than a hint of sarcasm in his voice.

The woman looked at him with a deer-like stare. "Nice shirt," she sneered while looking directly at his bulging stomach. The elderly woman was wearing a dull brown housedress and her gray hair was pinned in a neat bun. "I'm sorry, mister, we're out of eggs. We should have some by afternoon." Her voiced quivered from old age.

The detective stretched his arms out with palms up. "No eggs, how can you have no eggs?" He dropped his arms, put his hands on his hips, and quickly searched the shelves with his eyes. The detective grabbed a jar of Heinz dill pickles instead. "I'll take this."

The older woman put the glass jar of pickles into a bag. "All you want is pickles?"

"I wanted eggs," the detective said dryly.

"That'll be thirty-five cents." She handed him the bag.

The detective handed over the dollar bill and snatched the bag and coins from her without saying another word. He walked as fast as his pudgy legs would go soon driving off to the Sawyer's residence.

By the time he arrived, the pickle jar was empty.

# CHAPTER NINETEEN

Becky and Joseph walked out of the police station collectively taking a deep breath of fresh air. They had spent a lot of the early morning waiting in a small room with two chairs and a wooden table for the police sergeant to show up. When he did, they told him everything they knew, which ended up not being a hell of a lot. Becky let the officer know that coincidentally she had interviewed both of the victims for the local newspaper. The sergeant did not seem to care one bit about that or for that matter most anything they had to say. But he put up a slight smile nonetheless, thanking them anyway for at least finding the body. He then had politely sent them on their merry way.

As they headed for the truck Joseph attempted to hold her hand but she pulled it away. He tried again with the same results.

"Are you okay, Becky?" Joseph said.

"What? No, not really, I have a really bad headache. I

think I want to go home and lie down, but can you drive me to the drug store first?" Becky said.

"Of course. I'm really sorry you had to go through all that," he said.

Becky stopped walking to look up into his eyes. "I don't want to again."

"Sweetheart," Joseph said, "It's over, you won't ever have to, I promise."

"Then why does it feel more like a beginning to me?" She sighed a bit and tried to smile, but none was forthcoming. "You can bring me to the drug store first?" She repeated the question with a trace of pleading that Joseph did not catch. Her head was pounding and she simply wanted to be curled up on her bed, alone. It didn't matter if sleep would come or not. She wished she could reset the last couple of days. No. Reset her life.

———

No sooner than Joseph pulled his truck to a stop in front of the drug store, Becky took the few singles that were in her purse and jumped out. "No need to come in with me...I need girly stuff too," she said. "I'll be right back, Joey." In her wake her purse fell off the passenger seat and onto the floor. As Joseph picked it up a folded piece of paper slipped out. He had all intentions of putting the paper back into her purse, instead he read the first line that was printed on it.

These Words Are Not Mine

And even though he knew better he unfolded it and read every single word written down.

These words are not mine
I pluck them from the wintry air
seizing them as they drift down
from the sky
to cover my yearning
like the palest snow

These words are not mine
I draw them from the deepest river
they flow to me
filling me until I choke with scenes
and scents
of people and places I will never
know

These words are not mine
I pull them from the roots of the
trees
through the dark rich soil of the
Earth
where they fester in wounds
that will never heal

These words are not mine
I steal them from the animals
around me
squirrels and birds and deer
that flee to hide from my broken
heart

These words are not mine
I absorb them through my thirsty skin
from the sun as the warm rays melt
away my last thoughts
of a love I can never have

These words
they are not mine
but I will give them
to you

Joseph carefully put the paper into her purse. Through the store's front glass window he stared at Becky as she walked deeper into the establishment. She turned right and disappeared from his view.

Her words had unexpectedly touched his heart and he wiped at a tear that rested on his cheek. "My God, that was beautiful."

CHAPTER TWENTY

The Desoto engine had barely any time to rest when the naked girl, fully clothed, stepped out from the Sawyer's residence.

"I wonder where Mrs. Sawyer is this very moment?" the detective murmured. He intensely watched the woman as she haphazardly stumbled along the path. Suddenly she stopped, bent over, and threw up. The detective involuntarily cringed. The naked girl stood up took no more than two steps before bending over again. This time the detective looked away. Suddenly, the thought of her being naked wasn't as appealing anymore.

She got into a blue car and screeched out of the driveway with sparks flying as she steered the car landing hard onto the street's pavement. The tires squealed in a sharp turn.

"Shit!" the detective yelled and tried quickly to start his car. He flooded it with gas. His foot pumped and pumped on the accelerator while he kept one eye on the blue car speeding down the street. "Come on, come on, come on." The engine stuttered over and over again. As the blue car turned right about three blocks down the detective's car turned over. He kept his foot pressed on the gas pedal.

The detective drove to the third block and turned. He immediately slowed down. Not only did the naked girl catch a red light, she actually stopped for it. *Thank goodness.* He continued to follow her, keeping a block's distance as she drove across town.

She finally parked directly in front of a small tavern. Naked girl apparently knew of a bar that was already open or perhaps never closed. He waited a good half hour before she reappeared from the bar and walked much more sure-footed to her car. This time she pulled out at a normal speed.

She doubled back. About a dozen blocks later she stopped in front of a pay phone. The detective pulled his car over about a half block away. He wished he could hear what she was saying. But she seemed upset by the way she was moving her arms in the air as she talked on the phone. After the call, she sat in her car for so long the detective nearly fell asleep. More than a couple of times his eyes closed for a few seconds. Finally he saw the naked girl simply pull away. A few blocks later she stopped and parked her car. She got out and leaned on her front hood, posed like a model. Her legs looked extra-long and thin in the short shorts she was wearing. Once again the detective began thinking of her without clothes.

After passing her with his car, the detective parked his usual half block away and got out to look around. There wasn't anything special about the area. It was mostly apartment buildings with each one separated by an alleyway.

In the street at least eight young teenage boys swarmed around playing stickball. They were using chalked boxes for bases. The last kid at bat swung and missed, flinging the saw cut broomstick to the ground. None of them seemed to care a lick about naked girl or the cars passing by nearly hitting a couple of them.

The detective lit up a cigarette and took a couple of draws. "Now, the question is, who the hell is she waiting for?"

After snuffing out his fifth cigarette with his shoe it seemed that she heard something. She was walking straight into the closest alleyway.

"Okay, now we're getting somewhere," the detective said. He stayed on the other side of the street and started to lumber along the sidewalk.

"Hey mister!" one of the kids yelled. "Throw the ball back!" He looked down as the high-bounce ball had rolled close to his shoes. He picked it up and flung it to the kid closest to him.

"I use to play when I was I was younger," the detective said.

"They had stickball way back then?" the boy said.

"Yeah, kid. They even had streets," the detective sneered.

He made his way passed the alleyway trying to steal a glimpse from across the street. Besides naked girl, he saw another person at the other end of the alleyway, a female. After going a few more feet he crossed the road making his way to the right hand edge of the alley. He peered around the corner for only a second. "No way," he muttered to himself. He had to take a better look to make sure he saw who he thought he saw. He counted in his head to three looking around the corner again this time for a couple of seconds.

The detective was right, it was Mrs. Sawyer. She looked straight at him. Quickly she walked his way passed naked girl nearly knocking her down. "You were followed you idiot," he heard her scream.

Instead of going toward his car he went as fast as his legs would carry him to the next corner where a phone booth stood. He plunged his hand into his pocket, remembering he had coins there from the mom and pop store. The block was long and it felt to him as if it took forever to reach the phone booth. Not having the luxury of waiting to catch his breath he immediately slipped a quarter, the first coin he had grabbed, into the phone's coin slot. "Come on, come on, come on," he shouted at the phone's receiver.

---

One of the kids was about to pitch the ball but his arm stopped in mid-air. He stood like a statue staring and pointing beyond the kid with the stickball bat in his hand. "Did ya see that? Near that phone booth!" he squealed. "A car ran right into that guy."

"Yeah, right!" The kid with the stickball bat would not look. "Come on, stop fooling around, pitch the ball already! My mom says I have to be home for lunch!"

CHAPTER TWENTY-ONE

Becky walked passed the women's feminine hygiene products, straight to a bottle of Bayer aspirin. Her hand was shaking slightly as she opened the bottle up and poured four aspirins into her hand. One by one she dry-swallowed them.

"Okay, I'll feel better soon. Right," she said. "It says two aspirins will make me feel better. So I should feel twice as better." Becky giggled at her own words. She didn't know where the laughter was exactly coming from, but she couldn't stop. It soon became out of control. Tears streamed down her face. Her eyes burned. She tried to catch her breath. *What's wrong with me Mom? Maybe I'm just not ready to be away from you. Maybe, maybe I should go home. Maybe I don't have patience after all.* Thinking about her mother stopped her laughter cold.

To her left were boxes of Kleenex tissues. She grabbed a box, opened it, wiped at her wet cheeks and eyes, and blew her nose. She repeated it with two more new tissues before making her way over to the pharmacy counter where a gentleman stood with a crewcut, wearing a blue lab coat-style jacket. It appeared as if he watched her the whole way as she walked over to him. Maybe he even had caught her giggling breakdown, she wasn't sure. Becky *was* sure that a goofy smile was plastered onto his face.

Becky relinquished the opened bottle of aspirins and tissues to him. She couldn't help but think the employee looked a lot more like a science teacher than a pharmacist. She then handed him two dollars.

"What was so funny?" he asked as he handed her change and the two items now safely tucked away in a paper bag.

Becky looked over her shoulder to the area she had been in. "Oh, you saw that." She stared at him. "I really don't know." Her voice wavered.

"Are you okay?" the pharmacist asked. He then smiled broadly.

"Maybe not," she said as she shrugged. "You know, my life hasn't gone actually like I planned." *No, you don't know mister pharmacist guy, because I don't know you and you don't know me.* "What's your name?"

"My name's Walter…Wally."

"Well Walter Wally, I'm sorry, but I have to go."

"Wait!" He handed her a Hershey chocolate bar. "It's on me. My mom always told me that chocolate makes any situation feel better."

"That is really sweet of you," she said.

Becky hopped back into the truck, a third of the chocolate bar already in her mouth. "You know what Joey, chocolate does make you feel better, wanna bite?" She put the bar near his mouth and he took a bite of it.

"I'm glad you're feeling a little better, Becky," Joseph

said, "because I have to tell you, your poem accidently fell out of your purse and I couldn't help but read it. It was really beautiful. Sweetheart, you never told me you wrote poetry."

Any smile she had instantly vanished. She calmly shoved the last bit of the chocolate bar into the bag with her other items. "Take me home now," she voiced with no emotion.

"What?" Joseph said.

"Now," she repeated.

"What's the matter?" His throat became dry. Joseph had never heard Becky speak like that and his heart sank. "It's not because I read your poem?"

She said nothing.

"Really, you're mad because I read your poem?"

"Those were private thoughts. You weren't meant to read them. No one was meant to read them," she said curtly.

Joseph felt worse by the second. He couldn't believe that he had made the girl he loved so angry at him. "Listen, Becky, I'll make it up to you tomorrow, I'll—"

Becky finally turned toward him. "I'll be working at the newspaper pretty late tomorrow."

"Well, then the next day, I'll—" Joseph was cut off again.

"My working schedule is crazy for the next week or two actually," Becky lied, "I'll call you when things settle down."

Joseph silently stared into her eyes for a moment; he saw nothing in them that he recognized. He was beginning to feel lost in his own vehicle. "Becky, I'm really sorry I read your poem. What can I say or do for you to forgive what I did?"

Becky smiled politely. "It's fine. But I'm really tired."

"Right," Joseph whispered. He drove her home and watched her get out. He was going to say "I'm sorry" one more time but thought better of it, so he said nothing and neither did she. Not even goodbye.

Becky entered her apartment. Without locking her front door she rested her back against it for a few moments as if she were keeping the whole world from coming in. Her sights went toward the garbage can standing near her kitchen sink. She opened the lid of the trash can, grabbed her poem from out of her purse, and taking her sweet time ripped it to shreds, letting the pieces float aimlessly from her hand to the bottom of the trash.

She was feeling worse than she imagined she would about how she treated Joseph. She knew what she had to do next. Becky dialed her mom's phone number. She would tell her the day's strange events and maybe, just maybe, ask again what her sister was up to these days.

# CHAPTER TWENTY-TWO

*Three days later*

The typewriter sat dormant with a single piece of white paper curving out from it. Becky sat on a rolling chair at arm's length away from her desk staring at the inanimate object as if it might actually start typing something on its own. *Wouldn't that be a hoot.* That would make the front pages of her newspaper, of any newspaper in the country for that matter.

She always wore stretch pants and some kind of matching plaid shirt to work. She bought all the colors; today she felt like blue. Her boss had, on more than one occasion, strongly hinted for her to wear dresses. Becky cared not to take the hint.

She spun around on her chair. When she heard the click of the front door, she stopped immediately. The door opened and her boss, the editor-in-chief, strutted in, his usual thirty minutes late.

"Don't forget my coffee, pretty eyes," he said as he briskly walked past Becky and into his private office.

She wanted to say, *have I ever forgot, baldy*? "Coming right up, Chief," she said instead. It only took her a minute to bring him the coffee that had already been percolated. When she went into her boss's office he stood behind his desk already loosening his gray tie with one hand the other was holding a small piece of paper.

Becky placed the coffee down. She would have been surprised if he thanked her. There were no surprises coming.

"Do you have an assignment for me, Chief?" Becky nonchalantly asked.

Her boss fiddled around some more with his tie before finally taking it off completely and shoving it into one of his desk drawers with his other gray ties. "So, if your baseball boyfriend calls again today, am I still supposed to say you're busy and you'll get back to him another time?"

"Yes," she said bluntly. "Do you have an assignment?"

He ignored what Becky said as he glanced down at the paper he was holding. "So, pretty eyes, recognize the name Millie Alden?"

Becky pursed her lips together for a moment. "Of course I do, I did a little story a couple of weeks ago about the dozen cats or so she has rescued over the last couple of years. Very sweet elderly woman. Why?"

He placed the paper down on his desk. "Apparently she left the gas on after cooking and she died in her sleep."

"Oh my God!" Becky said putting the palm of both her hands over her mouth. "And all those cats. I can't even think about it."

"About that; I made a couple of phone calls," he said.

"The cats are fine. Oddly enough, they were found outside in the backyard. Safe and sound. I talked to her nephew. He has no idea how the cats got out."

"That's three…Bernie, Teddy, and now Millie," Becky said.

Her boss sat down. "I don't believe in coincidences. One person, fine. Two, maybe. Now three, I don't like it. Who else did you interview?"

Becky thought a second. "Well, the owner of the Mudhogs, Randel Sawyer. He was my first interview. Uhm, after him was Joseph and then there were at least three, maybe four others before Millie."

He gulped a big sip of coffee. "For starters, maybe you should find those names and give them to the police."

The phone rang and he picked it up quickly. "You've reached the Gazette. Yes I recognized your voice Joseph." Becky stood there and shook her head no. "I'm sorry Joseph, but she is very, very busy and she will get back to you as soon as she can." He recited the spiel dryly. There was a pause. "Yeah she's standing right here." Her boss put his hand over the speaking end of the receiver. "He says he's sorry and that he loves you."

Becky took two quick steps and ripped the phone from her boss's grasp. "Joseph, please don't call here. I need more time. Why? Because I'm telling you I do. I know how you feel, I'm sorry." She gently placed the receiver on the base.

"So anyway, the police are gonna think we're crazy," Becky said.

"Yeah, well, give it to them anyway." The chief uttered after swallowing more coffee. "I hate coincidences," he said under his breath.

*One week later*

Becky was escorted by the only woman police officer on the staff. Becky thought her eyes looked empty, perhaps too many years on the police force or perhaps she had a sister like hers. The husky woman in blue opened the door that had a large rectangular glass pane in the top half. It was the same small room with two chairs and a wooden table that she had been in with Joseph. She gave Becky a polite enough smile and left her alone.

Only a few minutes passed when a police officer entered the room, closing the door behind him. She immediately recognized him. It was the same sergeant. Today he looked a little worse for wear. Becky could only guess that his exhausted look was directly related to why she was here. He had a cigarette sticking out from the corner of his mouth. In each one of his hands was a cup of coffee. He placed one of them in front of her. "Here you go ma'am. I figured you could use a cup."

Becky looked at him with a semblance of a smile. She took a small sip. It tasted like it had been sitting in metal for days. "Thanks," she said, just the same.

The sergeant took his cap off long enough to rub his hand through his short, greyed crewcut hair. His dark blue uniform looked lived in for days. The cigarette hanging from his mouth wasn't lit. The sergeant plucked it out of his mouth and grinded it into the floor with his black oxford. "It's about time I put that cigarette out of its misery. I've been nursing that one all day, haven't had time to go get another pack. You wouldn't happen to have one on you?"

Becky sat in the chair shaking her head. "I don't smoke." She pressed her legs as close together as she could sensing she picked the wrong thing to wear today; her cream colored dress was a little too short for her liking. But no matter what she wore Becky was beginning to feel uncomfortable in a different way, as if she were being interrogated not questioned.

The sergeant sat down across from her. "Miss Taylor—"

"Call me Becky," she suggested.

The sergeant clasped his hands. "All right...Becky...is there anyone you can think of who would be doing this to you? Someone who might hate you enough?"

She tugged down on her dress some more and then rubbed her arms. "Don't you think if someone hated me that much, they would have just, I don't know, killed *me*?" Becky had the strongest urge to leave.

"Yeah, the problem, *Becky*, is we don't really know what to think and right now. Your 'Eyes on Farmstead' articles are the only common denominator we can see." Any friendliness in his voice was gone now. "When it comes to murder there is no rhyme or reason. For all I know, Becky, you might have killed all these people to become a famous journalist." She thought he must be kidding. At least she hoped he was.

Becky tried to kid too. "Yeah, actually I murdered them all to sell a few more papers so I can get a raise in pay."

"People have killed for way less," he said. This time there was no kidding in his voice.

Becky leaned toward him. "How come only a few days ago when I tried to tell you what was going on, you didn't believe me. And now two more people are dead, that makes five. It would have been six if Charles Holden hadn't left town on vacation."

The sergeant tried to grab a non-existent cigarette from his mouth. "Yes, I didn't believe you. I didn't believe there was a serial killer on the loose."

"And now?"

He scratched the top of his head. "And now I have men watching Joseph Tonti and Randel Sawyer, twenty-four seven. I have to ask you again—"

A police officer rapped on the closed door to get the sergeant's attention. He then nodded with his head for the sergeant to come into the hallway.

The sergeant stood up. "Excuse me a moment." He went over to the police officer and they both went a bit further away from the room. Becky heard their voices but what they were saying was mostly indiscernible.

A couple of minutes later the sergeant returned. He actually had a kind of smile on his face...maybe.

"It's over," his voice boomed in the small room making Becky jump.

"What's...what's over?" Becky said.

"It seems Randel Sawyer's wife and her cousin were behind an elaborate scheme, going after all of his money. The pressure must have gotten to the cousin because she ended up snitching on Mrs. Sawyer. Of course they blamed each other for the murders. Neither one wants to go to jail for the rest of their lives, I suppose. It'll be up to the courts to figure out what to do with them."

Becky's face paled.

"Are you okay, do you want some water?" He spoke softly.

"No, I...I just can't believe it." Becky shook her head.

"Well, if you come back later today we should be able to give you some kind of official statement for your newspaper."

The sergeant escorted her to the front door and held it open.

As Becky stepped outside she quickly turned. "Joey! I mean Joseph, is he all right? Do you know where he is?"

The sergeant grinned. "He's fine and he's safe now. He's actually down at the malt shop."

---

Joseph sat on the same stool he had been when she first met him. From Becky's angle inside the store, she could see he was nursing a milk shake. She quietly went over and stood about a foot behind him.

"I hear this place has the best shakes in town," she said trying to disguise her voice.

Joseph spun around in his chair. She gave him a tender kiss on the lips. "I'm sorry, Joey."

Joseph's eyes started to tear. "No, I'm sorry. I love you. I missed you."

Becky smiled. "Come on, let's go to your place. We can catch up on everything."

"My place?"

"Yes, your place." She took his hand and gently led him out of the store. As soon as they were outside he pulled on her hand to stop them. "I don't really care why the change of heart, I only care that you're here," Joseph whispered.

Becky smiled at him. "I was hoping. Hey, we need to stop at my place first, okay? I have to pick up a couple of things."

## CHAPTER TWENTY-THREE

Becky stood in the middle of Joseph's family room clutching dearly to a small pink overnight bag. She hadn't changed her clothing while she was at her place. There was no real reason to. She had actually thought a lot about this night for the last few days. Becky hadn't made her final decision until this moment. This very moment.

Her body shook and shivered, shivered and shook. She knew rubbing her arms this time would not relax her. Becky shook her head, she was beginning to think she liked Joseph too much. It scared her.

Without moving from her spot she glanced around impressed with how well the room was decorated, how clean it was for a single guy. She wondered if maybe a female companion had lived here at one time, having had a hand in the décor. Becky stopped her thoughts cold. Her mind then went in a totally different direction; *it didn't matter if someone had lived here before, all that mattered was—*

"Hey Becky! You like sweet tea right? I mean, who doesn't," Joseph shouted from the kitchen.

His words were squished together. *He's nervous too.* She then heard a refrigerator door closing.

"Becky! Sweet tea?"

She clutched her bag even tighter. "Yeah! Yes! Sure!" *There was no moving from this spot now.* Opening her bag she pulled out the only item that was inside. The only item she would need. A small revolver loaded with six bullets. She let the bag drop to the floor. *No sense concealing anything now, right Mom?*

Joseph walked into the living room with a smile, a glass of iced tea, and a small black jewelry box. *He's as ruggedly handsome as it gets*, she thought. For but a moment Becky felt a tug at her heart.

"I just can't wait any more to give you something, sweetheart." His smile dissipated in a heartbeat when he saw Becky standing there with a gun pointing right at him. Slowly a smile returned. "Okay, I'm not sure what kind of prank you're pulling but even pointing an empty gun is not really funny."

He took another step forward. The sound of the gun firing followed by the bullet hitting an oil painting on the wall behind him, sending it crashing down onto the floor, shocked him back into place. The glass of iced tea was no longer in his hand. Small pools of sweet brown liquid were all around his feet. Somehow the glass did not break but rolled across to where Becky stood. She kicked it away from her.

"It's-not-empty," Becky finally said. She barely recognized the sound of her own voice. Guessing from the look on his face, neither did he.

She shook her head. "I didn't want this, you know; I kinda liked you." She waved the gun in the air. "And what the hell is in that small black box? You didn't, did you?"

"Sweetheart, are you okay, are you drunk?" Joseph said.

"What? That's the only logical explanation? Booze?" She laughed low at first building in volume until it was nearly as loud as a scream.

Joseph took two quick steps forward. "Becky, sweetheart, it's all right, you're in some kind of shock from everything that's happened." He took a third step. "Let me —" The gun fired again. Joseph inhaled in pain. The black box fell from his hand in unison with the blood oozing from his left bicep. With his right hand he clenched on to the wounded area. The black box had opened and the engagement ring sat naked on the floor sparkling and glaring at Becky.

Her face filled with a mix of shock and disbelief. "Honestly? A ring?"

"I love you." Joseph murmured. Surprisingly to Becky, there didn't seem to be any anger on his face. It was…it was sadness. She was breaking his heart. No, she was shattering it. Witnessing that made her want to cry out. But she had to stay with the plan, even if it was plan B or C or any other letter you cared to come up with.

"I fell in love with you, Becky, you know that."

"Stop it! You know there's a bullet in your arm? You know I shot you? And you fell in love with me? You don't even really know me! What did you think, there would be a happy ending? That you could read me like a book? There was never going to be a happy ending with me, with the *Becky* story!"

The blood was spreading on Joseph's arm.

"Jeeze, sit down, Joey, or you're going to pass out."

Keeping his hand pressed on his arm he gingerly sat down on the couch.

Becky never stopped pointing the weapon at him. "Scooch on all the way over to the end." She waited until he moved then sat down on the other end. There was a smear of red on the top part of the couch where he dragged his arm against it.

Their eyes met for a few moments before Becky looked away. "I know what you're thinking, but I'm not crazy." She looked at her gun and then to him. "Well, maybe a little bit crazy." Becky smiled broadly. "I like you. I wasn't...I wasn't going to kill you, really." Becky shook her head. "But no, Sawyers' idiotic wife had to enter the picture, didn't she?"

"Sawyer? Randel Sawyer? I don't understand," Joseph said angrily.

"Right. You wouldn't understand, would you?" Becky figured. "Or maybe you would now that you know a little about broken hearts." She stood up and paced, being careful not to wander to close to Joseph. "You know, I would fall in love and then my lovely older sister would steal him. Not once, not twice, but every time." Becky chuckled. "My sister wasn't even that pretty. But she would do things I would never do with a boy. That's how she stole them, you know." Becky didn't know whether to scream or cry. "Stole...my so-called sister, stole my life from me. She stole my home."

Joseph continued to hold his wound while he spoke. "I'm sorry about your sister. You should have told me long ago."

"My mom would tell me 'have patience with your

sister, she would change'. My mother actually said that deep down she was a good girl," Becky said. "But I knew she wasn't going to stop until I stopped her."

"You need to let me go to the hospital," Joseph said and attempted to stand up.

She took a step toward him with the gun pointed at his head. "Don't! Please. I didn't get to the best part."

He stopped.

"Good. I left my home town, my sister, behind. I fell in love...completely. Funny, you know the guy. He was on your team. Eddy."

Joseph's eyes widened and for a brief moment he forgot about the burning pain that was consuming him. "Eddy Walker? But...he would never..."

"Cheat? Cheat on his pregnant wife. Yeah, think again. And because of Ran-del Saw-yer," she said, "he died on that bus."

Joseph cocked his head. "No. You? All of this killing... you? Just to kill Randel?"

"No Joey, not to kill him, I wanted him to suffer, I wanted him looking over his shoulder for the rest of his life. This is so cliché, but killing him was too good for him. So you see, he thinks it's over now. He's safe. He thinks his wife did all this." She took a deep breath. "I wasn't going to kill you, Joey...you have been so amazing to me, but I never loved you. I'm sorry, you happened to be next in line, that's all. If I kill you, Randel will fear for his life again. You see that right?"

A tear, then another, ran down Joseph's cheek. "I'm sorry too. I loved you so much. Dammit! Dammit...I still love you."

"How is that even possible?" Becky said. "Did you hear

anything I just said?"

Joseph slowly shook his head. "I don't know how it's possible. I wanted a life with you so badly. God, I never wanted anything more in my whole life."

Becky stretched her arms in front of her to the fullest, aiming the gun at his chest. "Close your eyes," she said.

"No."

"I don't want you looking at me! Close your eyes!" she demanded.

Joseph said nothing, keeping his eyes open.

"Fine." Becky moved her aim to where she visualized his heart to be. But all she could see was his eyes. Through the corner of her eye she caught the sparkle of the engagement ring. She bent over and picked it up, slipping it onto her finger. It fit perfectly. Of course it did. Were there feelings inside her for him? She immediately took it off and flung it across the room. "Some things were not meant to be."

"We could still have that," Joseph said.

Becky knew he didn't believe his own words. How could he? "No!" she finally said, once again aiming the gun at his chest. She stood for nearly a full minute. "I hate you!" she screamed, flinging the gun across the room, then ran out of his apartment.

Despite the obvious pain, Joseph jumped up and chased after her.

Becky heard him following. She had no idea where she was heading, she only knew she had to put distance between them. She could not bear to look into his eyes for another second.

Darting across the street, Becky never saw the car coming.

# CHAPTER TWENTY-FOUR

*Please nurse, help me*! Becky was certain she was able to manage an eye twitch.

The woman wearing the white and blue uniform came over slowly, bending down closer and closer to her patient. The nurse then simply propped another pillow behind Becky's head. She felt her head move as much as you feel things happen in dreams she supposed; although, with the movement of her neck far off there was a sharp pain. She thought perhaps it was a blessing she could not precisely feel.

The nurse scurried out of the room leaving only Joseph sitting with his arm in a sling, staring, sadly smiling.

*How many days have I've been here?* Becky wondered.

Joseph waited a beat or two and walked over to her. He leaned in and spoke low. "I know you can't hear me. At least I don't think you can." *There was that damn sad smile again*. "But I pray you can, Becky. Cause I want to let you know I haven't told anyone, anything you said to me. And

I won't. I don't know, I guess that makes me pathetic. Or maybe you honestly can't shut off emotions like a light switch."

A balding, grey-haired man in all blue walked in and Joseph immediately stopped talking, straightened up, and greeted him. They shook hands.

The man in blue spoke first. "How's the arm holding up?"

"It's a little painful, Doctor, but it's getting better," Joseph said.

"Well, don't you worry about it, next year you'll be swinging the bat as good as new," the doctor said excitedly.

"I'm not concerned about me," Joseph said as he stared at Becky. There was no smile now, only that sadness.

"I can tell you, it's a miracle she's alive. She won't be able to even move her legs for some time. But I expect her to walk out of here under her own power one day. I'm not saying it will be easy for her by any stretch of the imagination. She'll need crutches for a few months, maybe longer. Right now there were so many bones broken it's best to keep her on pain medication around the clock." He shook Joseph's hand again. "Well, see you at the stadium next year!" The doctor spun around and left the room nearly walking right into a woman who was coming in at the same moment.

The woman stopped in front of Joseph. She was wearing a black skirt and dark grey blouse more suited for a wake than a hospital. "You must be J T. I follow baseball a little." She pointed to Becky and then to him. "You two were close; I'm so sorry what happened. I can't believe she was hit by a car. The same thing happened to...I'm sorry." The woman covered her face with her hands.

Seeing who the woman was, Becky desperately attempted to shut her eyes from this waking nightmare.

Joseph handed the woman a couple of hospital tissues. He stared at her face. "You, uhmm, have me at a bit of a disadvantage, as the saying goes."

The woman blew her nose, tossing the used tissue in a small mesh garbage can. "Thank you." She glanced at Becky. "My name is Amelia Taylor. I'm her sister." She paused. "You look surprised."

Joseph shook his head and glanced over toward Becky. "Did I? I didn't mean to."

Amelia went over to her sister and gently caressed Becky's limp arm looking right into her eyes. "I'm so sorry this happened Rebecca. So, so sorry."

*No you're not! I could kill you now!* Becky screamed in her head. *I should have killed you then!*

Amelia rubbed her sister's arm one more time.

*Stop it!!!*

"I'm sorry, I should have at least tried to get in touch with you. But...she hadn't really told me much about her family," Joseph stated.

"If it hadn't been on the front page of the newspaper I might never have known." Amelia turned to him, briefly rubbing his good arm. "That's okay, I'm sure there were many things she did not tell you." She turned her sights onto Becky. "Forgive me Joseph, for not looking at you while I speak. It's been so long since I've seen my sister."

"No, that's fine. I completely understand," Joseph said.

"My sister...she always was jealous of me..." Amelia started.

*No Joseph! She's lying!* Becky attempted to cry out. *She's lying!*

"…and she always assumed I was going after her boyfriends. Which of course I wasn't. Joseph, I couldn't help but notice you studying my face. It is a little, shall I say, off. I've had a lot of plastic surgery to correct scarring. You see, a few years back, one night Becky thought I was flirting with her newest boyfriend. I was on our front lawn when she came at me like a wild woman. She pinned me down and wouldn't stop hitting my face. Mom was the only one home but she couldn't get her off me so she ran across the street to get help and was hit by a car. She was killed instantly. Our dad was never the same. He died about a year later of a heart attack."

"Oh my God," Joseph stammered.

"Joseph, I still love my sister, I know it was all a horrible accident. I know in more ways than one it was and has been hardest on her. I thought for sure she would have had a mental breakdown. She's a lucky woman to have you."

Joseph only nodded his head.

Becky needed to tell him the truth, her truth, all of it, good and horrific.

"Joseph there's so much I'd like to share with you, but I'm getting a bit tired." A slight smile crept onto Amelia's face. It was meant for Becky alone. "I think I should get going. I don't know how long it will take for me to find a decent hotel room." She wiped away invisible tears.

"No. You should stay at my place tonight. I insist," Joseph said.

Amelia's smile grew. "That's very sweet of you, honey,

but I might be here at least a week depending on how well my sister is doing."

"Its fine," he said, "you can stay as long as you need to."

"I don't know what to say. Thank you." Amelia slipped her arm through his. "The very least I can do is treat you to some food. Something tells me you haven't eaten much today. And there's nothing we can do here right now except stare at her while she sleeps."

Joseph glanced over at Becky. "I should stay a bit longer, but I am getting hungry and tired," he admitted.

"Good." Amelia turned one last time to look at her sister. "Joseph, I'm looking forward to getting to know you better—the man who had his heart stolen by my baby sister." She winked at Becky sickeningly. "Poor, poor, Rebecca."

The two left the room.

The desire to end her sister's miserable life intensified within Becky. She focused on her legs. After a few seconds, and accompanied with incredible pain, her legs moved nearly a half inch. She repeated it again as the pain worsened. Then again, and again.

*I do have patience, I'll show you, Mom.*


The End

# ACKNOWLEDGMENTS

Thank you to Vania Rheault for her assistance with this book. I appreciate your time, and all you do for the writing community.

# ABOUT THE AUTHOR

D.R. Willis is an avid reader and writer of thriller/suspense, and began early on by writing short stories designed to entertain his mother who had become ill due to diabetes. This led him to the love of the written word he has today.

Visit D. R. Willis on http://drwillisbooks.com and these other social media outlets:

www.ingramcontent.com/pod-product-compliance
Lightning Source LLC
Chambersburg PA
CBHW020738130626
46554CB00006B/2042